"Every George Baxt
Griffith movie, wit'
little sense of humor, would not h...
sive one-liners and verbal pratfalls along the way. Baxt's final
chapters tend to provoke alternating gasps of surprise and
whoops of hysterical laughter from his readers."

"One of the finest of modern satirists."

By George Baxt:

now available in a Crime Classic® edition.
**forthcoming from the IPL Library of Crime Classics®*

GEORGE BAXT

TOPSY AND EVIL

A CRIME CLASSIC®

INTERNATIONAL POLYGONICS, LTD.
NEW YORK CITY

TOPSY AND EVIL

Library of Congress Card Catalog No. 87-82445
ISBN 0-930330-66-8

Printed and manufactured in the United States of
America by Guinn Printing, New York.
First IPL printing October 1987.
10 9 8 7 6 5 4 3 2 1

*This book is dedicated to
four friends, in order
of seniority:
Robert Mackintosh, Elsie Steinberg,
Venable Herndon and Ursule Molinaro*

1

"Ocelot is coming!"

It was the third time that day the provocative
advertisement had teased the Negro detective.
Twice in the morning newspapers, now once in
the afternoon daily. It had teased him three times
a day for the past four days. Monday he dismissed
Ocelot as a new mouthwash. Tuesday he dismissed Ocelot as a new British hairdresser.
Wednesday he decided Ocelot was another dreary
spy spoof. Thursday Ocelot had titillating possibilities as the latest and lasting contribution to literature by Jacqueline Susann. ("Ocelot lay naked on
the chinchilla rug in front of the Venetian marble
fireplace, the reflection of the blazing logs illumin-
ating her perfect breasts like two unexplored
moons. From the corner of her eye she could see
millionaire sportsman Hymie Kodak circling her

9

like an astronaut. Did he suspect his would not be the first landing?")

But today, Friday, his speculations on Ocelot proved to be as pointless as an anecdote in Leonard Lyons' column. Today the ads carried a beautiful line drawing of the mysterious Ocelot. Ocelot was a lady cat. A singing lady cat. A singing lady cat with a gimmick. Her name was Ocelot and she looked like an ocelot. The drawing emphasized petite ocelot ears, an ocelot nose, and ocelot whiskers protruding from her upper lip. Two ocelot eyes peered sexily from behind what was very obviously a cleverly designed ocelot mask. Subtly, the drawing indicated Ocelot might be a colored lady.

"Hooray for our team," he muttered to himself as he flipped the page to Daisy Gotham's society column, where the lead paragraph drew his immediate attention.

I *love* a mystery, and doesn't everybody? It's exactly one year since stunning, gorgeous, much-sought-after Jo Alcott took mysteriously ill and disappeared from the swinging scene, and how our Jo could swing! We thought at first she'd gone into mourning for her good pal and frequent escort, the mysterious, ravishingly handsome international playboy, sportsman, financier (has anyone *ever* found out where all that money came from?) and good pal of kings, queens, dictators, presidents, television panelists, etc., etc., Guru Raskalnikov, who was so brutally murdered (and when will *that* ever be solved, if ever, I keep *asking* myself) just one year ago today. (Subtract five hours, all you darlings in London). I had a brief chat on the phone with Jo's equally stunning, gorgeous, much-sought-after mother, Topsy Alcott, whose chic and exclusive Tara Club is jampacked nightly with anybody who's anybody (don't you sometimes wonder why anybody would want to be *anybody?*) and much as I adore clever and witty Topsy, she was extremely reticent about discussing Jo's whereabouts or the state of her health. Do you suppose Mama Topsy has her hidden in the lavish triplex above the Tara Club—or maybe next door in the old Zoltan mansion in which the unfortunate Raskalnikov had his skull crushed last Christmas Eve? Heavens! Do you suppose *Santa* did it? On to cheerier things. At last night's opening of *Say Uncas!,* the musical version of *The Last of the Mohicans,* Anita Louise Berger and Arlene Francis . . .

The detective crumpled the newspaper in a sudden burst of irritation and flung it across the room at the wastepaper basket. *And when will that ever be solved, if ever, I keep asking myself.* We got that in common, Daisy baby. I keep asking myself the same question. I keep the file on the Guru Raskalnikov murder in the top right-hand drawer of my desk to remind myself it's still unfinished business. I loathe unfinished business. But I'm alone in wanting to clear up this murder. Nobody's exactly told me to forget it, but neither does anybody bug me to get the case marked closed. In fact, I'm convinced somebody up there prefers the whole matter be forgotten. Why? Where's the pressure coming from? Who's afraid of whom?

Who crushed Guru Raskalnikov's head with a blunt instrument? What was the instrument? What happened to the murder weapon? Did the murderer take it with him (her?) or did it just walk out of the room by itself?

Who *was* Guru Raskalnikov? Where *did* all that money come from? Was it true he had been an intimate of the late Serge Rubinstein's, also brutally murdered and the killer still at large? How important was Jo Alcott's connection with Raskalnikov? Had they been lovers, as rumored, or just friends? How much does Topsy Alcott know? Raskalnikov is murdered and Jo Alcott suddenly disappears from the swinging scene. That week, somebody else disappeared from the swinging scene. Is there a connection?

Where's Pharoah Love?

The detective placed a cigarillo between his lips and lit it. He exhaled a perfect smoke ring and then leaned back in the swivel chair, lost in thought. His mind went back to a day eighteen months ago. A warm, sunny June morning following a cold, bleak meeting of the Police Review Board. A meeting where certain charges against another Negro detective named Pharoah Love were "dismissed for lack of conclusive evidence" and Love conveniently resigned from the force. Love's roommate, novelist Seth Piro, after an argument with the detective, fell into a water-filled bathtub, bringing a live radio crashing down into the water with him and thereby electrocuting himself. Earlier, Piro had been a suspect in the ironically similar death (proven to be murder) of his former lover, male hustler Ben Bentley. Had Piro actually been Ben Bentley's murderer? Had Pharoah Love withheld evidence to protect Seth Piro? So alleged a brilliant book on the case published last Christmas, *In Cold Water*, by Peter and Robert Moulin.

The book was published December 20. Pharoah Love's disappearance dates from December 21. Guru Raskalnikov was murdered December 24. Jo Alcott took mysteriously ill and disappeared from the swinging scene on or about Christmas Day. Pharoah Love had been working as a bartender at the West Side's number one "in" spot, Ida's Place. Ida Maruzzi, proprietress, reported Pharoah Love didn't show up for work the evening of December 21 "and I had to work the *farshtunkener* bar myself until I got a replacement." Raskalnikov and Jo Alcott, either together or in the company of others, had been habitués of Ida's Place. And, occasionally, Topsy Alcott. What's the connection? Is there a connection? What about Jo's three sisters, Meg, Beth and Amy?

Who gave the word to soft-pedal the Raskalnikov investigation?

Who the hell *was* Raskalnikov?

The phone rang.

He stared at it.

The phone rang again.

He blew another perfect smoke ring.

On the third ring, he answered it. His voice was soft, well-modulated, and cultured without pretension.

"Satan Stagg."

The voice at the other end was pure tapioca pudding. "My name is Peter Moulin. Perhaps you've heard of my twin brother and myself. We wrote *In Cold Water*."

Satan didn't commit himself beyond "What can I do for you?"

"We're interested in the Raskalnikov case. Can we talk?"

"I'm listening."

"I meant over drinks or dinner or brunch or whatever is most convenient for you."

Satan took a deep drag on the cigarillo.

"Are you there, Mr. Stagg?"

Satan exhaled thoughtfully. "I'm here."

"Would drinks this evening be convenient? I realize it's Christmas Eve, Donder, Blitzen, ho-ho-ho and all that jazz . . ."

"I'll have to get back to you. What's your number?"

Satan jotted the number down on his desk calendar and then repeated it back to Peter.

"When can we expect to hear from you?" persisted Peter.

"Maybe an hour. Maybe less. You'll hear from me."

He hung up. Satan scratched his chin. Peter and Robert Moulin. Interested in the Raskalnikov case. A rueful smile played on his lips. The fickle finger of fate.

Peter Moulin replaced the phone in the cradle, sank back in the overstuffed Morris chair, and ran his fingers through his soft blond hair. He then lifted the very cool, very perfectly concocted daiquiri to his very cool, very perfectly concocted lips and sipped. His reasonable facsimile, Robert, was stretched lengthwise across the nine-foot-long cashmere-covered couch reading a letter, intermittently groaning or emitting an occasional "Dear God" or a weary "Toujours gai and whatthehell."

"Robert."

The brunet didn't stir.

"I said *Robert.*"

"Dear *God!*" Peter's twin turned over on his stomach and buried his handsome face in the pillow, his left arm clutching the letter dangling limply.

"I think our fears are well-founded," said Peter, "Mr. Stagg doesn't sound as though he'll be terribly cooperative." He sighed. "What could be worse?"

"Mother," was Robert's muffled reply as he made a feeble gesture with the hand holding the letter.

"Now what?" inquired Peter with a bland expression, "She fall off an alp or compromise a mountaineer in a snowdrift?"

Robert pushed himself up to a sitting position. "Let me have the dubious pleasure of reading it to you." He cleared his throat and then spoke in a voice that was pure chocolate mousse. " 'Hello hello hello-o-o-o-o!' "

Peter shivered. His twin's imitation of their mother's voice was perfect. Peter could almost see the glorious, glamorous never-to-be-forgotten former darling of the silver screen Madeleine Cartier wearing her ostrich-feathered negligee, standing by the fireplace waving a glass of champagne as she deliciously and delicately tried to expiate a recent sin.

" 'This is Mumsy, of course,' " Robert bearing down on 'Mumsy' with satirical exaggeration, " 'who misses you terribly and begs forgiveness for not having written these past eight weeks. Oh, darling darling darlings, Mumsy's cup runneth over' exclamation point exclamation point exclamation point."

"That cup's not running over, it's sloshing."

"To continue. 'I must start at the beginning, where of course all things start. There was lonesome little me in Rome being pursued up streets and down alleys by those loathsome *parapazzi* on their motorcycles with their cameras . . .' "

"Mother, of course, on horseback shrieking for the Pope."

" '. . . which eventually gave poor Gino a nervous breakdown.' "

"Who the hell's poor Gino?"

"I guess the jockey she met at Ascot."

"Continue."

" 'It was therefore necessary to bring Gino here to Gruyère, where he made a rapid recovery and disappeared with his night nurse six days after our arrival and I should have been highly suspicious from the moment she promised never to leave his bedside. Anyway, you know Mother. . . .' "

"Do we ever." Peter poured himself a fresh daiquiri.

Robert crossed his legs and continued. " 'Easy come, easy go. Then the most fantastic thing happened. A cable from Germany offering me a role in a German-Italian-Israeli-Australian co-production to star Hardy-har-har Kruger' exclamation point exclamation point exclamation point and a coffee stain. 'I decided if I accepted the role I ought to do a bit of rejuvenation of the type darling Jean Arthur and some of the other girls did before attempting their comebacks. It just so happens that right here in Gruyère is the famous Goldberg Rejuvenation Clinic and certainly you have read in Time magazine all about Goldberg's variations. Well, darlings, to make part of this long story short, Mumsy has spent the past six weeks being rejuvenated. Actually, I think they went a bit too far and now I think I'm all wrong for the part of Hardy-har-har's evil sister. I look more like his evil daughter' exclamation point exclamation point exclamation point and will you pour me one of those damn daiquiris and stop being a pig?"

Peter poured the daiquiri and carried it and his to the couch, where he sat next to his brother.

" 'But that's the least of why I'm writing. Oh, my darlings, my babies, my own sweet angels, Mumsy has at last met Mr. Right . . .' "

"Exclamation point exclamation point Exclamation point."

"Exclamation point killer." Robert sipped his daiquiri and then returned to the letter. " 'And when I tell you his name you'll simply die. Archimedes Zoltan!' "

Peter's chin dropped. "Archimedes Zoltan!"

"In living color."

Peter faced Robert. "And Raskalnikov was murdered in Zoltan's mansion."

"Well, you can't blame Zoltan. It was a sublet."

"You know damn well what little facts we've gleaned about Raskalnikov point to some sort of suspicious alliance with Zoltan."

"I do know damn well, so shut up and listen to the rest of this." He lit a cigarette and returned to Madeleine's letter.

" 'Arkie, as I now call him, comes to the clinic once a year for treatments and for once my timing was just right. He didn't pay much attention to me before my treatments, but when I slipped out of my bandages—wow.' "

"Wow."

" 'And all along I used to think Archimedes Zoltan was some terribly old ogre who controlled the purse strings of the universe and built and destroyed empires and governments and created wars and arranged assassinations and is still suspected as the brains behind the disappearance of Judge Crater. Well, let me tell you, he's just a cuddly little teddy bear and he's asked me to marry him and I said yes and couldn't you both die though I trust you're in the best of health.' "

"More daiquiri?"

"To say the least."

"Continue reading while I mix."

" 'Think of it, darlings, think of it—me, Madeleine Cartier, Mrs. Archimedes Zoltan. Won't that bring all of stinking Hollywood to its knees' and ten exclamation points. 'Zoltan has promised me two magnificent wedding presents. He plans to buy Metro-Goldwyn-Mayer for my very very own and of course I plan to replace that damned lion at the opening of every movie with me me me. And wedding present number two is the dearest gift of all. He promises to spring Flora and Fauna, your darling misunderstood grandmother and aunt, from the Women's Rehabilitation Institute in upstate New York where they never deserved to be sent for murdering Sweet Harriet Dimple who was a pain in the ass anyway if you'll pardon my French.' "

The bottle of rum Peter was holding slipped from his hand and crashed to the floor. "I'll wipe it up later. I haven't the strength now. Is there more?"—pointing to the letter which now trembled like a leaf in autumn in Robert's hand. Robert nodded.

" 'We're returning to the U.S. in about a week or so, or as soon as Archimedes finishes some business in Germany with somebody named Kurt Georg Kiesinger, whoever that is. We'll be staying at his mansion in which he says somebody or other was murdered last Christmas Eve but as you well know Mother has no superstitions although I get the feeling this person who was murdered was almost like a son to Archimedes.' "

The twins' eyes met.

"Almost like a son," whispered Peter, "yet the powerful Mr. Zoltan seemingly has done nothing to bring Raskalnikov's murderer to justice. Robert—the letter isn't as dire as I thought. Now we get into the Zoltan mansion. We get to know dear Archimedes himself. Robert, it's a stroke of luck."

"I haven't finished this yet," said Robert dully.

Peter sank into the Morris chair.

" 'Archimedes is arranging for one of his dearest friends, Topsy Alcott, to give us a huge party New Year's Eve at this exclusive club she runs called Tara. Archimedes says Topsy knows you two. Something to do with your spooking around with some idea of writing a book about the death of this somebody or other last Christmas Eve. I know the name but I can't spell it. Archimedes says it's the name of some character in some book by some Russian and you know I never read books especially by Russians especially since that terrible McCarthy mess who surprise surprise was a dear friend of Archimedes. Anyway, my own darling precious angels, Arkie wants only one wedding present from you two dear generous angels: Don't write the book. Thank you thank you thank you. Much much much much love. Your devoted mother Madeleine Cartier,' and you know what to do with your stroke of luck." The letter fluttered from Robert's fingers to the floor as he stretched out again on the couch.

A depressing silence hung heavily over the room.

"Robert."

"What?"

"We're going to promise to drop the book."

"I thought you'd say that."

"But we were always a pair of stinkers, Robert."

Robert sat up swiftly with a delighted grin. "I thought you'd add that. Are we seeing Stagg or aren't we?"

"He said he'd call back within the hour."

"He'll call."

"You're so sure."

"I'm very sure."

❧

Satan Stagg shut the door of his superior's office, crossed the hall and entered his own, shut the door, crossed to the swivel chair and sat staring out the window. Now I know for sure. The suspicion's been gnawing at my innards for a year, but now I know for sure. They don't want the case broken. They don't want Raskalnikov's murderer. They let me waste a year on the damned case knowing damned well there'd be no damned results. Didn't Pharoah hint shortly after he resigned it was something similar to this that helped him shield Seth Piro as Ben Bentley's killer?

❧

It had been shortly before the cocktail hour at Ida's Place. The waiters were scurrying around setting tables. Ida was in the kitchen barking orders at the chef and his staff. Satan sat at the bar sipping a martini while the slim and lithe Pharoah completed his setups.

"It was all going for me, cat," said Pharoah, neatly arranging a row of shot glasses, "because the Ben Bentley cat had a lot of important names in his little black book, names powerful enough to put the pressure on. So they accepted the murderer I handed them. Anything to help make the case yesterday's news. And Seth was in the clear. I'd still be in the clear if it wasn't for those frigging twins."

"What happens when their book comes out?" Satan asked.

"I don't know, cat. But just in case, I got a little plan." Pharoah grinned his magnificent grin. "It's way way out—but what isn't these crazy days? Listen, you're new and you've got a lot to learn. Lots of cases get quashed like this—"

Two people walked in and called for dry Rob Roys, and Satan never heard the rest of Pharoah's sentence.

≈§§≈

Satan lit a cigarillo, opened the top right drawer in his desk and took out the folder on Guru Raskalnikov. It was an extremely thin folder as murder cases go, and that in itself gave Satan a depressing, debilitating feeling of inadequacy. Damn it, he swore to himself, when I made detective I swore I'd give better than my best to this job. I only owe to one person. Me. Satan Stagg. Satan reached for the phone, read the number he had jotted down on his desk calendar, and dialed.

2

THE WOMEN'S REHABILITATION INSTITUTE occupied three acres of land abutting the Hudson River, which, an observer once remarked, seemed to flow past with an air of embarrassment. The two hundred and forty-three inmates, though female, were hardly ladies. They served their sentences under an honor system set up by an earlier warden, a spinster lady of a really good Buffalo family who had graduated with honors and a biology professor from Bryn Mawr, and, upon her retirement from W. R. I. some two decades earlier, published her memoirs, *Bad Girls Don't Have Babies* (three printings, despite few ads, and the Catholic Book Club, which didn't find out the former warden was an Episcopalian until after the deal was a *fait accompli*) and then settled in Barbados, where she became a holy terror among the natives whom she insisted must call her "Bwana."

W. R. I. had been the recent "in depth" subject of a television network show which had barely skimmed the surface, and it had once made the cover of *Sports Illustrated*. Its present warden, Mad Myrtle MacGruder, a former Roller Derby champion and vegetarian, was even more lax in her administration than its innovator. "Don't blame my kiddies," was Mad Myrtle's frequent comment when confronted with disciplinarian problems. "Blame society and stop putting so much vermouth in my martinis."

Mad Myrtle's kiddies occupied fairly spacious cells, three kiddies to a cell, in which they could curtain their barless windows, keep Kewpie dolls and transistor radios, and decorate their walls with photographs (mostly Robert Mitchum, Colette and Jess Stearn), samplers (such as "Jesus Watches When the Screws Ain't," "Remember to Write Mother, It Gets Lonely in Dannemora Too," and in one cell "God Bless Johnson and Johnson") and the *Playboy* calendar.

Christmas Eve at W. R. I. was just like Christmas Eve anywhere else. There were brawls, fist fights, attacks with lethal weapons as Christmas trees and inmates lit up.

Lights out was usually at 10 P.M., but this holiday eve some cells had lights out as early as 8 P.M. due to smashed bulbs and slashed wires. Only in one cell did serenity reign. The cell was unusual in that it was furnished in beautiful and immaculate good taste, two of its occupants having been in a position to exert some outside pull. One wall was decorated with stills from such classic early movie musicals as *The Barclay Mill Follies* of 1929, 1930, 1931 and 1932. There was a photograph of the late Barclay Mill himself, whom one of the inmates of the cell had murdered over three decades earlier by blandly breaking his neck. There were photographs of such Barclay Mill starlets as Madeleine Cartier, Zelma Wave, Sweet Harriet Dimple and Flora and Fauna Fleur. There was a more recent photograph of Sweet Harriet Dimple, a rare one secured after much difficulty from private police files. It was Sweet Harriet hanging by the neck from the branch of a tree in Central Park where two of the inmates of the cell had placed her.

Another wall of the cell had been decorated by the third inmate. There were autographed photos of Emperor Hirohito, Tojo, Sessue Hayakawa and Douglas MacArthur. There were also pinups of Toshuro Mifune, Sylvia Sidney as Madame Butterfly circa 1932 and Peter Lorre as Mr. Moto. There was one sampler sewn, and with great pride, by the inmate herself: "When in Doubt, Use Karate."

The inmates were Flora Fleur, a large, powerfully built woman in her middle sixties, her petite and pretty daughter Fauna, who was fourteen years her junior, and a squat, bulky, not unpretty American-born Oriental once known to American G.I.s as the infamous Hiroshima Hattie, but better known to her cellmates as Winnie Ruth Judo. The three sat on their cots by the light of a transistor lamp. Flora was knitting a sweater, Winnie Ruth puffed on a cigarette that projected from a five-inch jade-encrusted holder, and Fauna pored intensely over a group of playing cards neatly dealt adjacent to a letter received that morning from her sister, Madeleine Cartier.

"Well, baby," said Flora to Fauna with warmth and affection in her voice, "what do the cards tell you?"

"Cards rie," hissed Winnie Ruth. "You can't terr the future by them rousy cards."

"Shut up and let Fauna concentrate," snapped Flora. "You have to let the deck warm up. Fauna's been getting waves all day, ever since we read that letter from Madeleine. Nothing in the cards yet, Fauna baby, about that Archimedes Zoltan?"

Fauna shook her head impatiently. "Give it time, Mother."

Winnie Ruth hissed, "Try reshuffrring."

"Stop upsetting Fauna."

"Me?" said the suddenly astonished Winnie Ruth. "I never upset nobody. My motto is 'Rive and ret rive.' "

"*You*," snorted Flora as she caught a stitch on the verge of dropping. "Buddha wouldn't melt in your mouth."

"Baroney."

Fauna peered closer at the top row of cards she had dealt and then uttered a faint but unmistakable moan. Flora leaped to her feet and Winnie Ruth tensed.

"What, baby, what?" cried Flora. "What do you see?"

"Madeleine," whispered Fauna. "It's coming through for Madeleine. I've been misreading the cards. I've been looking for Archimedes Zoltan, but it's Madeleine spread all over these cards. Look.

Look right here—the queen of hearts. That's Madeleine." Flora and Winnie Ruth were now huddled next to Fauna. "On the left, the king of spades . . ."

"Zoltan?" It was Flora who spoke.

"Zoltan." Fauna nodded. "And on the right of the queen of hearts . . ."

Flora gasped and eased her left breast to one side to clutch at her heart. "The ace of spades!"

"Death," whispered Fauna.

A shiver shinnied up Winnie Ruth's spine and she drew her obi tighter around her jasmine-colored kimono. As often as she scoffed at Fauna's fortunetelling predictions, just as often did she have to admit to herself Fauna was often "infarribre." Only last Thursday, Fauna had advised against eating the soup at dinner that night. It was after her second helping that Winnie Ruth learned the cook had held her assistant's head in the tureen until she promised to stop stealing her LSD-coated sugar cubes.

"Terr us more," whispered Winnie Ruth.

Flora clamped her wrist in an iron grip. "Don't push my baby. Let it come natural."

"Above the queen of hearts," whispered Fauna, "the jack of spades." She turned and looked into Flora's mottled face. "Murder."

Flora released her grip on the wrist as Winnie Ruth hissed, "Horribre."

"Go on, baby," said Flora, voice trembling and eyebrows arched. "What does the spade trey under the queen of hearts mean?"

"Help."

"Herp?"

"Yes, help," said Fauna to Winnie Ruth. "Help must come in threes when one is surrounded by evil spades."

"There's three of us."

Fauna and Winnie Ruth stared at Flora. A sly smile slanted across Winnie Ruth's lips.

"You're wercome to join me when I break out of this dump."

"It won't be easy," insisted Flora.

"I get in," said Winnie Ruth with a dramatic shrug of the shoulders, "I get out. Nisei come, nisei go."

Flora turned to Fauna. "Redeal 'em, baby."

"*Why?*" said Fauna petulantly, reminding Flora of that day that seemed like centuries ago when she had told Fauna they'd have to murder Sweet Harriet Dimple. "The cards don't *lie!*"

"I know they don't, baby," said Flora affectionately, patting Fauna's cheek. "Read 'em for us. If the cards tell us to go with Winnie Ruth—" she paused and took a deep breath—"then we break out of here with Winnie Ruth."

"Better hurry and shuffre," said Winnie Ruth with a cryptic smile as she settled back on her cot and lit a fresh cigarette. "Boat to freedom reaves on Sunday."

"Boat?" Fauna was staring wide-eyed at her mother.

"Boat," repeated Winnie Ruth with a smile. "Sunday we row against Hunter Correge. If you decide to reave with me, two members of my team wirr have upset stomachs and you two rovries wirr reprace them. Reave it to Winnie Ruth Judo."

"But Mama," said Fauna with a petulant whine, "we're up for parole next month."

"Parore!" scoffed Winnie Ruth.

"Winnie Ruth's right," said Flora. "Shut up, baby, and shuffle."

❧

"Mr. Stagg," said dulcet-toned Peter into the phone, "you've proven it once and for all. Yes, Virginia, there is a Santa Claus. Eight o'clock at Ida's Place." He hung up and turned to Robert. "Now, why were you so positive he'd call back?"

"Because he's Pharoah Love's protégé," explained Robert as he adjusted his ascot in the mirror.

"You're still so positive the missing Pharoah cat is in some way linked to Raskalnikov's murder."

"Something he knew made him take a powder."

"It was our book and only our book."

"A minor excuse," said Robert as he crossed to a sideboard and began mixing daiquiris. "He knew months before the book was released that we had the facts and had every intention of publishing them. Why'd he wait until on or about December twenty-first before vanishing into thin air like Alice's Cheshire and, unlike that ephemeral animal, taking his grin with him? No, brother," as he turned the switch on the blender, "Pharoah was marking time until the moment of departure was propitious. As the everobservant Ida told us, he'd gotten rather chummy over his months of bartending at her pub with the likes of Raskalnikov, Jo Alcott, and the formidable Topsy. Ida suspects there was a bit of a kadoodle between Pharoah and Topsy." He switched off the blender. "And where there's a kadoodle there's fire."

Robert crossed to Peter, handed him a fresh daiquiri, then sat Indian style on a large ottoman. "Let's go over what we've managed to glean to date on this case."

"We've gleaned damn little."

"Exactly, and stop being so dense. That in itself is an extremely important clue. Four days after the murder was committed and made headlines, it abruptly disappeared from every newspaper in the country. Even our powerful gossip columnists stopped printing their tantalizing little tidbits hinting that if a murderer were brought to justice the ensuing scandal would rock the world. Let's begin with the victim. Guru Raskalnikov. Who was he?"

"International financier."

"When did he first become newspaper copy?"

"According to our intensive research, approximately a decade ago."

"On or about the time the mysterious Serge Rubenstein was murdered." Peter nodded. "What do we know of Raskalnikov's origins?"

"Damned little."

"Exactly. In France it was claimed he was a Rumanian prince. In Italy he was identified as a Bulgarian count. In Israel they charged he was a militant Arab. In other words, you has your pick and you takes your choice. He traveled on nine passports. He lived a lavish existence, yet we've been unable to pinpoint his source of income. He was romantically linked a dozen times a year with heiresses, actresses and members of royalty, but of the seventy-three women we've interviewed the majority refused to talk either out of discretion or out of fear, and we agreed fear was the more likely of the two, but inevitably, by listening closely between the lines, all roads led to Topsy Alcott."

"Who simply smiles and says, 'Why don't you two sweeties forget about it and have a drink on the house?'" He tapped cigarette ash into a porcelain tray and sipped his drink. "And where there's smoke there's fire. For smoke read Topsy Alcott, for fire read her eldest daughter, Jo." He placed his drink on the table and rested his chin on the palm of one hand.

Peter took over the conversation with alacrity. "And very suddenly, on or about Christmas Day, Jo Alcott acquires a mysterious illness, disappears from the public eye and to this day remains sequestered, in, we assume, a room in her mother's triplex above the Tara Club. Is the reason genuinely a mysterious illness, or is she perhaps being guarded against her will because she knows too much, or . . ."

"Or is she dead?" interjected Robert with a provocative lilt.

"Or is she dead." Peter stared into his daiquiri, but no answer to the whereabouts of Jo Alcott manifested itself. He plinked the lip of the glass with thumb and index finger and looked at Robert. "Now we come to the Zoltan mansion and Archimedes Zoltan." Robert nodded slowly. "And Mother's letter"—Peter trembled slightly at the memory of its contents—"confirms several of our darkest suspicions. There was definitely a link between Raskalnikov and Zoltan, and the all-powerful Zoltan could very well be the man who's pulled the switch that's caused this sudden blackout of the investigation of the Raskalnikov murderer. Robert."

"What?"

"When the lovebirds return to this country, they'll be living together in the mansion. Hardly proper," Peter commented, a sly tinge of irony coloring his voice, "considering they've not yet been joined in unholy wedlock."

Robert's eyes and spirits brightened considerably.

"I do think," continued Peter, "that you and I insist we join them under that roof as chaperons. Don't you agree?"

"The motion is definitely seconded."

"And with any luck," said Peter with a smile of self-content, "we'll be domiciled in the room in which the late unlamented met his tragic end."

"We can dream, can't we?"

"Oh, we'll swing it all right. We don't know Zoltan, but we do know Mother. She's the high priestess of togetherness."

"We'll consider it settled. Let's get back to Topsy and her ménage." Robert drained his glass and handed it to Peter for a refill. He clenched his left fist and then, in order, uncurled each finger. Thumb. "Topsy Alcott. Who is she?"

"Proprietress of the Tara Club, New York's most chic, most exclusive, most expensive." Peter and the freshly poured daiquiri gurgled in unison. "She appeared from out of nowhere a little over three years ago—"

"Precisely," interrupted Robert, "like another famous Topsy—she jes' growed. She appeared from out of nowhere with four extremely individual young beauties whom she introduced, publicized and exploited as her four daughters. The four young ladies proceeded to undertake a campaign to woo and perhaps win four of the wealthiest, most powerful men in this country, a campaign that was rumored to have sent Joli Gabor and her brood to their respective boudoirs with cold towels pressed to their heads. So far, neither of the four young chicks has chalked up a marriage, though our impression is they're waiting for someone to give them the signal—then watch for a sudden rash of 'I do's' by at least three members of the Alcott clan, assuming Jo might have been permanently scratched. Had Raskalnikov been Jo's intended?"

Peter had handed his twin the fresh daiquiri and settled down on the sofa. "Possibly," said Peter. "When Topsy opened her club, at a time, we must remember, when most other major New York City clubs were either near-empty or folding due to the unfortunate recession and tightness of money, she, contrary to the prevalent conditions, flourished like a hothouse orchid. She books the top, frequently unobtainable-to-others-at-any-price talent, and they play for whatever price she offers them. She rules society with an iron fist and a rapier-swift tongue, and I find her absolutely ravishing."

"Yes, Peter," acquiesced Robert. "As Grandma herself might have said had she met Topsy, 'What a piece.'"

"But as to who's backing Topsy, who's the power behind her well-upholstered throne, who helped her acquire that previously unacquirable and highly desirable property that houses her club—conveniently adjoining the Zoltan mansion, I add with what I hope is an appropriate air of piquancy —there isn't a clue."

"Yet." Robert nailed the word into the conversation with the force of a triphammer. "We now gently nudge Topsy to one side and take under consideration Meg, Beth, Amy and Jo. Jo is the eldest, a stunning blonde, no more then twenty-six or twenty-seven years of age. Next in line we have Meg, she of the jet-black hair and phony Boston accent, possibly a year younger than Jo, but with a face that bespeaks Irish lace, leprechauns and the Abbey Theatre. No so Jo."

"Definitely not so Jo," mused Robert. "Hers is the face of a Viking daughter that speaks of smorgasbord, fjords and the midnight sun." He leaped from the ottoman and began pacing the magnificently furnished room with its trio of twinkling crystal chandeliers. "And Amy. Neither Viking nor biddy. Amy's olive skin and almond eyes conjure up visions of bamboo huts, voodoo, and an entrance line akin to 'I am Tondelayo.'"

"Which leaves Beth." Peter blew out a match

and drew in on his freshly lit cigarette. "Beth is casting couches, posing nude for calendars, brandy alexanders and the B.M.T. subway. And there can't be more than a year's difference in their ages. Those girls couldn't possibly claim the same father."

"If they do, I'd like to find the man and donate him to science."

"Now," said Peter in a voice that commanded attention, "the murder of Guru Raskalnikov." Robert stopped pacing, rescued his glass, then crossed and sat next to Peter. "Guru Raskalnikov, age anywhere from mid-thirties to mid-forties depending on which paper you read, is found brutally bludgeoned to death in the bed of his stunningly furnished private chamber on the second floor of the eighteen-room Zoltan mansion. The death chamber overlooks the garden. The windows were locked from the inside without a trace of fingerprints. In fact, nowhere in the room was there a trace of fingerprints, especially . . ."

"Oddly enough . . ."

". . . of Raskalnikov himself. Meaning that shortly after the murder whoever did it had sufficient time to wipe the place clean. Even blood and bloodstains were exclusive to the bed itself. According to the coroner's report, which for the moment we must accept as reliable, the death occurred sometime between midnight and one A.M. Christmas Eve—or Christmas morning, if we wish to stretch a point. The skull was brutally crushed by a heavy instrument, said instrument having seemingly vanished into thin air. Forensic tests of

35

other heavy objects in the room revealing not a trace of blood or hair or skin or whatever the hell forensics are supposed to reveal. On the other hand, Guru Raskalnikov's very strange, very weird, very personal valet . . ."

"Now conveniently in the employ of Topsy Alcott . . ."

". . . a rather strange little man who boasts of a broken neck that now causes him to hold his head at a sixty-degree angle, and who answers to the name Igor Isogul, reveals in a rare, harried and unguarded moment to a very persistent reporter from *Newsweek* that his master was still *alive* when he found the body at approximately ten minutes to one, and that before expiring thirty seconds later the victim whispered one word."

Robert whispered the word.

" '*Rosebud.*' "

3

BY THE TIME the twins reached the subject of Igor Isogul, Robert had exhausted the five fingers of his left hand and the thumb of his right, and weird Igor was now represented by the right-hand index finger, which Robert wigwagged like a semaphor as he whispered for a second time, *"Rosebud."*

"A nickname, perhaps," suggested Peter. "Which of the five Alcott lovelies do you suppose might be called Rosebud?"

"Perhaps Mr. Raskalnikov in a rare moment of black humor chose to leave the world on a cloud of whimsy," said Robert with a bemused expression. "When 'Rosebud' was Orson Welles's dying word in *Citizen Kane*, it represented the sled he played with as a child."

"Well, then, which of the five Alcotts owns a sled?"

Robert had resumed pacing. "Let's get back to Igor Isogul for the moment. Somehow, he appeals to me as a prime suspect. Here is a strange little creature who quite openly and with great pride admits he was hanged by the neck as a traitor to his country thirty years ago, miraculously survived the punishment and couldn't be retried or rehanged because theoretically he had paid his debt to society. Then, a twenty-year gap in his history. We know that at some point he left his native Transylvania and wound up in the employ of Guru Raskalnikov as his personal valet."

Peter was now positioned in a near-perfect reproduction of *The Thinker*. "And after Raskalnikov's murder, in a seemingly generous and benevolent gesture, Topsy Alcott immediately places Igor in her own employ as butler. It's all too smooth, Robert, much too smooth." He straightened. "It's all so well-organized, so precise, never a break in the continuity. It puts our own meticulousness to shame."

"Peter." Robert was at the window, staring out at but not seeing the Manhattan skyline. Peter was gently massaging a throbbing temple. "Peter, though Raskalnikov's murder, the actual violence, was undoubtedly the work of one person, I am convinced the actual plot was the work of several people." Robert turned and faced his brother. "Wheels within diabolical wheels, so to speak, the work of a gigantic human computer—and, as in all computers, somewhere there's a flaw. If we could only find that flaw."

Peter groaned. "I can't think any more. I just

can't. My brain feels as though it's about to burst. So many loose threads. So many blind alleys. Could Igor have been lying about finding Raskalnikov with one last breath in him? Perhaps 'Rosebud' is a red herring. Could the connection between Raskalnikov and Zoltan be a mere coincidence? If Zeckendorf were murdered in England, would we go on the trail of J. Paul Getty? Why does Pharoah Love's disappearance cloud us with suspicion? And Jo Alcott. Each a separate alley of its own. And where do all these alleys lead?"

"To the main thoroughfare," said Robert gently, "Topsy Alcott, of course."

❧

The fingers that held the frayed article clipped six months earlier from the theatrical trade paper *Variety* were long and gracefully tapered. The fingernails were beautifully manicured and lacquered with a strikingly effective beige polish. The digits were devoid of jewelry. Precious gems would have detracted from the beauty of the hand, the perfect symmetry, the smooth swansdown skin which many a lip had hungrily kissed. The eyes, the cool ice-blue eyes, had scanned the article dozens of times in the past six months, but each reading revived the pleasure and delight of the first encounter.

NEW ACTS
OCELOT
Songs
25 minutes

If a gimmick alone were all, Ocelot would more than have it made. As it is, this cat-garbed (ocelot, what else?) femme backs up the striking and effective masquerade with a set of lusty pipes and a sexy delivery that had this predominantly male audience meowing for more. Ocelot mask covers three quarters of this sepia siren's face, the mystery adding in spades to chanteuse's allure. Remainder of costume is a neck-to-toes ocelot leotard complete with neo-phallic ocelot tail which serves as a useful prop. Songstress's movements are lithe and sensual and audience interest never falters. Opens with a saucy "What's New, Pussycat?" and then segues into a sequence of cleverly chosen pop and show tunes. A top booking in all situations and apparently being groomed by Topsy Alcott for her posh New York Tara Club. Only dubious lapse in taste at this showing occurred when audience gave femme a standing ovation and she responded by shrieking into the mike "I am the most!"

The fingers gently and with loving care placed the frayed article in the center drawer of the Louis XVI desk, closed the drawer, and then interlaced with the fingers of the other hand.

Topsy Alcott leaned back in the chair and shut her eyes for a moment, attempting to unravel a tangled skein of troubled thoughts that had plagued her for over forty-eight hours. Ocelot's opening New Year's Eve. *Ocelot is coming!* A brilliant campaign, she thought with unabashed pride as she embraced herself. New Year's Eve. Zoltan's cable. Huge party New Year's Eve. Zoltan and intended bride. Madeleine Cartier. The corners of Topsy's mouth drooped. He *would* choose New Year's Eve. He *would* choose to marry that tired sex symbol. Everything was going so smoothly until *this*. Well, maybe not all that smoothly, but nothing that I, Topsy Alcott, the shrewd, the invincible, the brilliant, couldn't cope with. Jo. Unfortunate. Igor. Time will take care of Igor. The Moulin twins. That book will never be written. Madeleine Cartier. The twins call her Mother. I call her many things, but a lady such as I never repeats them, especially to herself. My restless little chickadees, Meg, Beth and Amy. Money hath charms to soothe the savage breast. Ocelot. *"I am the most!"* Topsy smiled. She's been taught to feed her audience instead of her ego. Ida Maruzzi. *Where's Pharoah Love?* Where indeed is Pharoah Love? Raskalnikov. Tonight is the anniversary of his death. Should I have Igor light a *yurtzite?*

Meg. Faithful, clever little Meg of the raven hair, the raven mind and the raven heart. The blaze in her eyes when Topsy had read her Zoltan's instructions received earlier that day.

"You cahn't let him do this to you, Topsy! You cahn't!" Hands on hips, gorgeous little Meg was strolling back and forth in Topsy's Belgian-lace boudoir as Topsy sat in her peignoir serenely buffing her nails.

"Zoltan calls the shots, pigeon, and his aim is

faultless." Gorgeous Topsy, all five foot eight of her, with a flawless beauty no artist could accurately capture on canvas.

"If he marries anyone, he should marry you. It's ghahstly!"

Topsy, who was rarely given to shrugs, shrugged. "It won't last."

"Lahst is the *least* of it! Once she's his wife, she shares his bed, his home, his money, Gahd help us —and his confidence. What if she shares his *confidence?* Then where are we?"

"Pigeon, Topsy will handle everything in her own inimitable way. Now go have your mud bath."

Then Beth. Dizzy, scatterbrained stereotype blond Beth.

"Holy peroxide, Topsy, did you figure on this when we made the deal?"

It was half an hour after Meg had submerged in the man-made mire. Topsy was settled in her recliner chair with a damp cotton pad on each eyelid.

"Beth lovey," said Topsy in a voice that was pure nard, "there are seven long days until the intended marriage. So much can happen in seven long days. Remember the incident last year in Mexico City?"

"Holy chihuahua, supposing he'd married *that* bitch."

"But he didn't, did he? She was a clever piece of baggage, but Topsy arranged everything to perfection, didn't she? Now go have your pedicure and let me scheme."

Olive-skinned, sloe-eyed tantalizing Amy had slithered into the room ten minutes later, clutching the voodoo doll in one hand and a hatpin in the other.

"Say the word and she gets it right in the eyeball."

"Amy," said Topsy gently, "you're too old to be playing with dolls. I know you're dying to do that voodoo that you do so well, but I insist you obey me and destroy that obeah."

"I've come a long way from Saint Thomas," said Amy as she picked at her teeth with the hatpin. "We were promised wealthy, powerful husbands. Why the holdup? How long do you think my John will last? He's over eighty and he has to be spoon-fed his pablum. Does all this mean the plans are being changed? Do I go back to manufacturing gypsy love potions?"

Topsy stepped out of her satin-decorated dressing room, where she had changed into her Mackintosh original, and confronted the troubled Amy. She crossed to her and put her hands on the girl's trembling shoulders. Amy didn't raise her head.

"Look at me, Amy," said Topsy with gentle affection, "and none of that hypnosis nonsense. What did I promise my girls three years ago?"

Slowly Amy lifted her head. A tear was trickling down her cheek.

"Look at me, Amy."

Amy's eyes opened and met Topsy's. "You promised us the world."

"Have I ever reneged on a promise?"

"Never."

"Then we'll leave everything in my more than capable hands, right?"

Amy nodded.

"Now go to your room," said Topsy with a loving smile, "have your facial, and please stop burning nail parings and chicken feathers in your fireplace. The smell permeates the entire building, the odor is execrable, and you're far too intelligent to continue indulging in these primitive practices."

Christmas Eve. Topsy stirred in her chair. Not the sort of Christmas Eve I knew as a child. Was I really a child? Was I ever a sweet, wide-eyed innocent? That's all over and done with and it must be forgotten. I am Topsy Alcott. I am a powerful, adored, feared, vivacious and brilliant creature. I have my scheming cut out for me these next seven days. New Year's Eve. Ocelot's opening. The party for Zoltan and his . . . fiancée. There's Jo to be taken care of and . . .

She looked up as the huge oak double doors opened and the ugly little man with his head bent at a sixty-degree angle shuffled in, wringing his hands like Uriah Heep, with a vixen smile on his face. Topsy's eyes narrowed, the muscles on her face tensed and her hands formed knuckle-whitening fists.

Through clenched teeth she spoke with a threat in her voice. "Igor-r-r, how often have you been told to knock before entering?"

The expression on the butler's face did not alter. She recognized the mockery in his eyes. Slowly he spread his hands apart and spoke in his guttural voice with its trace of Central European accent.

"But Igorrrr did knockkkk, mahdommmmm. Perhapsss Mahdommm wassss preoccupieddddd."

Topsy had a strong urge to break his neck which she quickly quelled upon realizing she'd already been beaten to it. "What is it?" She clipped each word like a dead branch.

"The catererrr and his wife awaitttt yourrrr pleasyoor."

"Send them in."

He made no move.

The insolent little monster. The digusting, disfigured, dreadful little monster. He sidled closer to the desk, wriggling sideways like a snake.

"Mah-dommmm recallsssss thisss issss Chrissstmasss Eve?"

"Would you like a chorus of 'Jingle Bells' to prove it?"

"Perhapssss Mah-dommmm hassss forgottennn Igor'ssss late massterrrr alwayssss gave Igorrrrr hisss bonusss on Christmasss Eve?"

"You'll get your bonus tomorrow along with the rest of the staff."

His upper lip curled. "Igorrrr issss speccccciallll."

Topsy's face was now an implacably serene mask. She settled back in the chair with one eyebrow arched and a Mona Lisa smile. She tapped an index finger lightly on the desk top, and when she spoke her vocal tone was a brilliant blend of Lynn Fontanne and William F. Buckley, Jr.

"A year ago, Igor, when I took you in out of the rain, so to speak, and placed you under my protective umbrella, I warned you not to go too far. Igor, it's a year later. You've gone too far. You continu-

45

ally test my patience. Learn this now and never forget it. *Topsy* is special and Igor is *nothing*."

(Those eyes. Those evil, mocking eyes.)

"Igorrrr issss . . . *immortallllll*."

"Don't let that broken neck kid you. I might decide to have it reset."

He leaned forward ominously. "Igorrr mightttt talkkkk."

Topsy shook her head slowly from side to side. "Igor won't talk. Igor knows better than that."

"Igorrr isss nottt frightenedddd."

"Nor is Topsy. Now send in the caterer."

They spent twenty seconds staring each other down, and then Igor finally turned and shuffled to the double doors and beckoned to the man and woman waiting in the outer hall.

The man was probably sixty years of age, if not more. He was tall and willowy and wore his blue hennaed hair in a modest little pompadour. He wore a tight-fitting gray-with-pink-pencil-stripe suit that was cut British style, and in his lapel there was a gentle sprig of lilies of the valley. The woman with him was about fifty, short and plump. She wore a billowing brown pleated skirt that was uniquely dotted with mayonnaise and ketchup stains. Her blouse was peacock blue with bolero sleeves, and its stains, if one ventured close enough to examine them, were dried whipped cream, margarine and cream-of-mushroom soup. She had a gentle, wistful air about her, an air as gentle and wistful as the Empress Eugénie derby she wore on her head. When Igor beckoned, she popped the last of a chocolate-covered cocoanut candy bar into her mouth, chewed twice and swallowed. The man took her hand, squeezed it, and led her into Topsy's office.

Igor closed the doors, chuckled under his breath and shuffled toward the wide circular marble staircase that led to the upper two floors of the triplex.

Topsy arose with a lavish smile and crossed to the man with her hand extended.

"Mr. Rachel!" She correctly pronounced it "Rahshell." "It's been so many months!"

"Hasn't it, though!" His voice sounded like a bos'n's whistle piping an admiral aboard ship. He shook Topsy's hand and then put his arm around the dumpy little woman. "I don't believe you've met my wife. She simply insisted on meeting the one and only Topsy Alcott. Mrs. Alcott—my wife, Ruthelma Kross, the celebrated literary agent."

"Ohhhhhhhh," chirruped Ruthelma, "so *this* is the legendary *creature* herself. But you're so beee-*yooooo*-tiful!" She shook Topsy's hand, and several seconds later, when the opportunity presented itself, Topsy wiped the chocolate from her fingers.

"Won't you sit down?" said the gracious Topsy.

Mr. Rachel selected a straight-back Queen Anne chair and Ruthelma sank ("submerged" was the word Topsy used later in describing it) into a love seat.

"I've a big job for you, Rachel. A very big job. And there's only seven days in which to accomplish it."

The caterer drew himself up haughtily. "And when has Rachel never risen to the occasion?"

"New Year's Eve" said Topsy, "five hundred

guests, downstairs in the club. A gala celebration for . . . Archimedes Zoltan—" Ruthelma's gasp did not escape Topsy's ears—"and his future bride, Madeleine Cartier."

"*Heavens!*" Rachel and Topsy stared at Ruthelma. "I *mean* . . . her *sons* never *mentioned* to me their *mother* was *bethrothed*. I wonder if they *know*."

Topsy sat behind the desk and then leaned forward with her hands clasped. "You represent the Moulin twins?"

"They're my *prized* possessions. I *sold* the best seller *In Cold Water*. And *now* they're researching the murder of Guru . . . ooh . . . ooh . . . ooh . . ."

"Exactly. Guru Raskalnikov. Ruthelma—" the smile that accompanied the agent's name was angelic and beatific—"may I call you Ruthelma? I feel as though we might have been Girl Guides together."

"Oh, *do* call me *Ruthelma!*"

"Ruthelma, the twins have been frequently advised to abandon this project. Shouldn't a word to the wise be sufficient?"

Ruthelma abandoned an effort to cross her legs. The effort gave her time to think, gather together all her mother-hen resources, check her ammunition and ride pell-mell into battle when the ambitions of her clients were being challenged.

"Any *murder* case is public *property*," said Ruthelma in a very precise but very friendly tone of voice. "I *mean*, if every *author* who'd been asked to *abandon* a project had *complied* with the *threat*" (Topsy stiffened, and Ruthelma was pleased at having scored a point so soon), "some of the *great* works of *literature* would have been *lost* to *posterity*. Such works as *Ecstasy and Me, My Life with Charlie* and *The Carpetbaggers*. No-no-no-no-*noooo*, Topsy—may I call you *Topsy?*" She cocked her head like a pouter pigeon. Topsy nodded stiffly. "It is my job as Peter and Robert's *agent* to *encourage* them, just as I *commiserate* with my darling *Rachel*"—gently jerking a chubby thumb in his direction—"when a baked *alaska* collapses on the *serving* tray." She smiled her most piquant smile, which was like the parting of a hot-dog roll. "After *all*, murder will *out*. What's everyone so *afraid* of?"

"It isn't so much fear," said Topsy briskly, "as the injury it might do to so many innocents."

"Well, everyone's *innocent* until proven *guilty*." The non sequitur hung over Topsy's head like the sword of Damocles.

Rachel cleared his throat, and Topsy's search-lights focused on him. She smiled. "Dear, dear Mr. Rachel, I bring you here to discuss my New Year's Eve gala and have the bad taste to ignore you with this pointless little discussion on a matter in which you have no interest whatsoever."

"Anything that concerns my precious Ruthelma interests me greatly," said Mr. Rachel politely and firmly.

"Of course. Shall we begin with the menu?"

A piercing shriek tore through the apartment, then another, and then still another.

Topsy leaped to her feet and rushed for the

doors as Ruthelma struggled out of the love seat and waddled to Mr. Rachel's trembling side. "Don't be *frightened*, sweetheart. *Ruthelma* will *protect* you!"

Topsy rushed up the marble stairs and was met on the landing by Meg, Beth and Amy.

"Jo's room!" shouted Meg.

The four women sprinted up to the next landing in time to see a door at the far end of the corridor fly open and Igor shoved roughly into the hall.

From inside the room, the four women as they rushed toward it could hear a whimpering "*Urgle gurgle urgle urgle gurgle urgle gurgle*." In the doorway brandishing an iron poker stood a nurse, whose face, normally as starched as her white uniform, was now contorted with rage.

"You've been told to stay away from her!" she shrieked. "The next time I catch you in here I'll crease your skull with this!"

Igor shuffled backward four steps. "Igorrrr friendddd. Igorrrr no hurtttt Missss Joooooo."

"Igor!" Topsy's voice snapped like a bull whip. "Go to your room. This *instant*."

Igor turned and shuffled toward the back stairs. Topsy and the three girls pushed past the nurse into the bedroom.

"Jo," whispered Topsy, "baby, baby, you've had a fright. Topsy is here, and all's right with the world."

The pathetic creature was huddled on a bearskin rug in front of the fireplace, clutching the bear's head and weeping. Topsy knelt next to her and lifted her gently, held her tightly and, rocking back and forth slowly, crooned a Swedish lullaby.

Amy spoke to the nurse. "How'd he get in here?"

The nurse leaned the poker against a chair and smoothed her uniform. "I went to the linen closet for fresh sheets. I don't think I was out of the room two minutes—"

"Jo is never to be left alone!" Topsy cut in sharply.

The nurse drew herself up stiffly. "I'm sorry. It will never happen again."

"Come, Jo," said Topsy gently, "come lie down." Jo permitted herself to be lifted to her feet and led to the bed. Her eyes were glazed and her skin was pale, but her translucent Viking beauty was as predominant as the Christmas star. Her flaxen hair hung to her shoulders, and her clinging negligee emphasized curves the Grande Corniche would have envied.

"*Urgle gurgle urgle gurgle.*"

"Lie down, darling. Stretch out. Nurse will give you a sedative, won't you, Nurse."

"I'll prepare it immediately." She crossed to the bathroom.

Topsy dismissed the three girls. "Go to your rooms." They filed out promptly as the nurse returned with a glass of powdery liquid. Jo lay with her eyes shut. Topsy turned to the nurse.

"What was Igor up to?"

"He was asking her a question."

"*What* question?"

" 'Where is Pharoah Love?' "

Topsy rose from the bed slowly and stared at the floor. Then she raised her head and locked eyes with the nurse.

"Has Jo had any lucid moments today?"

"None."

"You're sure."

The nurse nodded.

"But she must have understood Igor if she became this frightened."

"Well, Mrs. Alcott," said the nurse, "we've learned from past experience that certain things do get to her. Certain words, certain names bring a reaction."

"Has she had any pain?"

"Not that I could tell. Usually she signals by holding the back of her head. Then I can tell the area where she suffered the blow is troubling her. Actually, until Igor, it's been a quiet day except for the occasional gush of urgle-gurgles."

"See that she's not disturbed. If you need me, I'm in my office. I have visitors. Make sure she takes that sedative."

The nurse watched Topsy leave the room, shutting the door behind her, then swiftly crossed to the bed, placed the glass on the night table, and raised the girl to a sitting position.

"Jo," she whispered softly, "Jo."

Jo's eyes opened and stared ahead.

"We're alone now, Jo. Are you tired?"

Jo blinked her eyes twice.

"No. Good girl." The nurse smiled. "Shall we go on with our lessons?"

Jo blinked her eyes once.

"Good girl. You're a fighter. We'll find out who did this to you. Your mother's trying to hide the facts, but we want justice to be done, don't we?"

Jo blinked her eyes once.

"Yes, murderers must be found and brought to justice. I hated my brother, but I was glad when his murderer got his. To think I almost fell in love with the man, but that's another story. When you're well again, you can read it all. *In Cold Water*. The boys who wrote that book are trying to write one about Raskalnikov."

"Urgle gurgle."

"Don't get upset. Just listen. Your mother's trying to stop them. That's a sin. What's more important, it's a sin against you. The murderer tried to kill you too, but that never got to the papers. But so help me God, you darling angel, I'm going to help you relive and reconstruct that awful night and name that murderer or my name isn't Ada Bergheim."

4

AFTER Rachel and Ruthelma left, Topsy sat quietly with her arms folded on the desk, her head resting on her arms. Now I know, she thought to herself, now I know how Talleyrand must have felt when affairs of state were going contrary to his plans. But what was it Hitler used to scream before he had to make do in a bunker? *Divide and conquer.* Topsy sat up abruptly, her ice-blue eyes blazing with enthusiasm, her reinvigorated blood throbbing with anxiety, her brain issuing emergency orders to every nerve in her body. Oh, Jeanne d'Arc, had Topsy Alcott been advising you during that infamous inquisition, you'd never have participated in that barbecue.

She flipped a switch on the intercom and spoke crisply and authoritatively. "I'm changing Ocelot's opening. It's being moved up. Wednesday night."

"But, Topsy," came Meg's voice with its pseudo-Brahmin accent, "that hahdly gives us time! What about the newspapers, the ahdvertisements, and supposing Earl Wilson and his B.W. have other plahns that evening?"

Topsy's voice held Meg's ears in a steel grip. "Opening Ocelot New Year's Eve would conflict with Zoltan's celebration. We can't afford to take the play away from our discovery. Wednesday night. Now get busy. And, Meg—see to it that my personal invitation is sent to the Moulin twins."

"Topsy . . . I'm frightened."

"Darling," said Topsy smoothly, "as I once told Winnie Churchill, you have nothing to fear but fear itself."

"I thought you told that to Roosevelt."

"After I told Winnie." She flipped off, sat back in the chair, hands tightly gripping the end of each arm rest, head held high, arching her swan's neck regally, her face the determined face of a movie star demanding alimony.

Yes, Ocelot. *We* shall overcome.

❧

The Silver Zephyr jet plowed through the electrical storm over Greenland like an arrow shot by Hiawatha. The pilot and copilot, former astronauts who handled this mere aircraft like a kiddy car, checked their instruments, then clinked glasses and downed their slivovitz. Behind them, in the magnificently decorated cabin which ran the length of the craft, Archimedes Zoltan sat in his throne chair and patted his safety belt reassuringly. His huge leonine head, with its impressive face dominated by a Julius Caesar nose, the skin pure alabaster and unwrinkled, a chin so square and strong it would send a surge of envy through Kirk Douglas, the eyes two highly polished agates, and the strange little mouth looking like an indentation made by an early-Pompeian cooky cutter, faced a door on which a tiny red light shone over the word "Occupied."

She's in there, he thought to himself, and his body glowed with the delicious warmth of love. She's in there. My delectable wife to be, my Cleopatra with her body of an Aphrodite and 1934 Shirley Temple face. No, my precious Madeleine, Goldberg did not go too far. I love your new cherub's face, I love this new youth of you, I love the way you outbubble champagne and the way your brilliant eyes light up as though each were charged with a thousand volts when I mention my vast and now even to me incalculable wealth. I love the way you gush with unabashed pride when discussing your homicidal mother and sister and your sons— His face darkened. Your only flaw, my dear. Those lamentable twin offsprings sired by the late Barclay Mill. But then, you will look gorgeous in black.

Guru.

Zoltan's sigh made the curtains tremble.

Guru. Where did it all go wrong? What caused your dissatisfaction? I gave you the world and you ended up dribbling it like a basketball. And your deplorable finish. Crushed like a tsetse fly by a white hunter on safari. Who will be my new

Guru? Where will I find another like you and like Serge? It's been a year. And a year without a Guru is like a year without a right arm. Longer.

He didn't notice the tiny red light extinguish and the door fly open.

"Hello hello hello-o-o-o-o-o-o!"

Madeleine Cartier stood in the doorway, face wreathed with a seductive smile, cheeks newly dimpled and hair ablossom with tiny pink curls, a magnificent replica of Shirley Temple.

"Come sit at my feet, my beloved." Zoltan's voice was his one misfortune. It sounded like a piccolo being played by an asthmatic.

Madeleine skipped to his side, sank to the Persian-rugged floor, took Zoltan's hand and kissed each finger like a gourmet finishing off a plate of spareribs.

"Was I too long?" she whispered.

"You are never too long," he tweeted.

"Arkie." Madeleine's voice was unusually sober. "I've been thinking."

Zoltan braced himself.

"It's the boys again and this Raskalnikov book." She looked up at the impressive face and wondered why it suddenly seemed to go gray. "They're very brave, very stubborn, very strong-willed boys. Supposing they refuse to abandon the project. Will this have any bearing on our relationship?"

Zoltan took her left hand and rubbed the diamond which was the size of a golf ball in the ring on her fourth finger, and then stared thoughtfully at the emerald-and-ruby bracelet in the platinum setting. "They must do as they are told."

"Well even if they *do* agree to give up the book," said Madeleine petulantly, "what if someone else comes along and writes it and makes all those oodles of money that rightfully belongs to my boys?"

"The book will never be written."

Madeleine shifted and rested against his knees. "I don't like the threat in your voice, Arkie. It frightens me. You sound like one of my former lovers who now lives exiled in Sicily, where he's doing very well in heroin. You're filling me with dread. It's as though . . . as though you're saying if the boys go against your wishes you would . . . you would . . ." She couldn't finish the sentence, not because she had run out of words, but because she didn't want to voice the horrifying suspicion she'd harbored the past two weeks.

Gently Zoltan patted her head, the pink curls quivering like coiled springs.

"There are many ways of suppressing the truth," Madeleine. And it doesn't necessarily require melodramatics."

Madeleine decided to shift gears. "What about Topsy Alcott?"

"A rare creature."

"Yes, I'm sure she's rare, but supposing she doesn't cotton to me. There was a lot of gossip back at Goldberg's about you and Topsy. I gather she's a very jealous woman."

"Jealousy is for ballerinas."

"Oh, I can handle women," said Madeleine loftily, "but a rare creature is something else. Anyway," she continued cosily, "I'll have Flora and Fauna to comfort me once you spring them."

Zoltan's eyes narrowed. "You intend for them to live with us?"

"Only until they're rehabilitated. Isn't that what you're supposed to do with ex-cons? Besides, when you buy M.G.M. for me, I want my comeback vehicle to costar my mother and sister. We'll open with the three of us reprising our great number, 'Let's All Stick Together.' Boy, did we wow 'em with that one!"

Zoltan closed his eyes, and his fingers began to twitch.

But Madeleine was oblivious to this. Her thoughts were with Flora and Fauna and Peter and Robert and marriage and Topsy and New Year's Eve and a mansion in which Guru Raskalnikov had been murdered one year ago tonight, and she didn't realize she was clutching Zoltan's antique pendant which he had placed around her neck earlier that evening.

I've got a premonition. A horrible, horrible premonition. But what exactly is it?

"Arkie," said Madeleine slowly, "I'd like some bubbly."

≈§§≈

Ocelot stared at her mask reflected in the dressing-room mirror.

Wednesday night. Gangway, world, get off of my runway. Here comes Ocelot and she plans to wrap up the big city and stuff it in her bosom. She smiled, baring a superb set of ivories.

"You are the most, sweetheart," she whispered to her reflection. "You bought yourself a new life, a new world, a new career, and it's the best investment you ever made."

She picked up a lipstick and began tinting away with subtle strokes.

Okay, Topsy. You say Wednesday night and Wednesday night it is. No, Topsy, I'm not afraid. I don't know what fear is any more. I belong to me now and to no one else. The ones that could possibly give me away we can take care of. The one I have feared the most I now have where I want him. I am no longer afraid of Pharoah Love.

There was a sharp rap on the dressing-room door, followed by "Five minutes, Ocelot."

"Five minutes my ass, kitten," she shouted through the door. "Ocelot's got a whole lifetime!"

❧

Satan Stagg walked up Columbus Avenue toward the seventies and Ida's Place. His tall, broad-shouldered, athletically proportioned body defied the biting December wind with a black cashmere coat, muffler and gloves. Sparks flew from the ember in the bowl of the pipe firmly clenched between his perfect teeth, and his handsome face with its hazel eyes ignored the tacit invitations signaled him by the women he passed in the street. He dwelled on women frequently, and of late agreed with his Aunt Hattie it was time a man of thirty contemplated marriage. But tonight his mind was on a marriage of another sort. A marriage of minds. A marriage of information. A wedding that might result in the unmasking of a murderer. He thought of Pharoah's advice given the night before his friend and mentor had disappeared. "Never go against your better judgment, cat. And follow through, regardless of what them higher-ups tell you. Once you start groveling in the face of authority, you are no longer your own man. That's what my Seth baby wanted to be. His own man. I understand that now. Too late, I understand that."

Oh Christ, Pharoah, where are you? How I could use you now. Why haven't any investigations turned up a trace of you?

❧❧❧

In most places on Christmas Eve it was peace on earth and good will to all men. Ida's Place was bedlam. The bar was packed one hundred deep and there wasn't an empty table in the place. A gaudily decorated Christmas tree gasped for air in one corner of the large room, and the jukebox quivered with a cacophonous rendition of "Rudolph the Red-nosed Reindeer" sung by the Psychedelic Seven. On the postage-stamp dance floor a dozen mods and rockers jerked, frugged and monkeyed, and, surprisingly, everyone seemed oblivious to Ida's latest innovation, bottomless waiters.

An eighteen-year-old hooker in a mod skirt wedged her way to a group of five men at the bar and twitted hopefully, "I'm told this is a tow-away zone."

A balding young man with a beak nose hovered over a table and hopefully asked, "May I join you?"

"Membership's closed," growled a balding novelist with a look of distaste.

An oversized middle-aged woman in a sleeveless dress and a wart on her nose whispered in a young man's ear, "I've got something special for you for Christmas." The young man clutched his crucifix and said two Hail Marys.

In the farthest corner of the room, opposite the Christmas tree, at a table next to a door leading to Ida's newly constructed private quarters, sat Peter and Robert. Peter glanced at his wristwatch. "It's after eight. Do you suppose we're being stood up?"

"I doubt it," said Robert as he toyed with his daiquiri, his eyes scanning the crush of bodies in the room. "He may be here right now, trying to cut his way through that wall of human flesh."

"He may not recognize us. We should have told him we'd be clutching roses in our teeth."

"He'll know us," said Robert confidently. "We're the only two in the place with an air of distinction."

The door to Ida's private quarters were flung open, and out came Santa Claus.

"Ho ho ho ho ho!" roared Santa Claus. "Merry Christmas! *Joyeux Noël!* Ho ho ho ho ho!"

"Ida," said Peter, "you were never lovelier."

"Shit," said Ida as she pulled out a chair next to Peter and sat down, "nobody's paying any attention." She tore off her beard and signaled to a waiter. "Bring me a beer, Charlotte." She reached into her red jacket, pulled out a cigar and lit up. "You two alone or are you expecting somebody?"

"A Negro detective" said Robert.

The cigar and the hand holding it began to tremble. Peter reached out and patted the hand gently.

"No, Ida. Not Pharoah. Satan Stagg."

"Oh." She dragged on the cigar and was momentarily lost in thought.

"You still adore him, don't you?" said Peter.

"Yeah, the bastard. I was really beginning to get hooked on him. But what the hell," forcing a smile to her lips, "it wasn't in the stars. Still no trace, huh?"

Peter shook his head No.

"Beats hell," said Ida. "Disappearing like that. No goodbye. No nothing. Just gone, as though some auctioneer banged his gavel and yelled 'Sold.'" She shook her head sadly. "Why do they always keep walking out on me? I spend three months at Arden's Main Chance, lop off ninety pounds, change my hairdo, and look at me. No takers. And they promised me life begins at fifty-four. I ought to sell this joint and move to Majorca. How's the new book coming?"

"Like salt-water taffy through a tea strainer," grumbled Robert.

"As my grandfather used to say, it'll all fall into place. Just make room for it to drop." The waiter brought her beer and she gave the bottomless one a rough shove. "Wave it in somebody else's face. I seen better."

63

Robert's face brightened. "This must be Satan Stagg."

Peter and Ida turned.

"That's him," said Ida, and Robert and Peter got to their feet and in turn shook hands with the young detective. He exchanged polite greetings with Ida, who made a move to go.

Robert's hand restrained her. "Stay a few minutes, Ida. You might be useful in helping to collate our material."

Satan hung up his coat and sat down, and Charlotte appeared at the thunderclap snap of Ida's fingers. Satan ordered a seven and seven and then applied a match to the dying ember in his pipe bowl.

"I am here," he said between puffs, "at the risk of my career."

"We can top that," said Peter, "with our lives."

"No vivid writing, Peter," admonished Robert, and then he smiled at Satan. "There's more to the Raskalnikov case than the publication of a book about it. There's Pharoah Love's disappearance, for one." Satan nodded in agreement. "There's this sinister underground plot to brainwash any investigation of the case. And for us, my brother and me, there's the added complication of our harebrained mother pledging her dainty hand in marriage to Archimedes Zoltan."

"Merry Christmas," murmured Ida.

The waiter brought Satan's drink, and then the four hunched conspiratorially over the table.

"Let's try to begin at the beginning," said Peter, "and to our minds that means Pharoah's disappearance. Ida, we presume the last you saw of him was the night of the twentieth."

"That's right." She wiped beer foam from her mouth with Santa's beard. "How did he act? How did he behave? I know you've already told some of this to Satan months ago, but Robert and I just might detect a clue that escaped Satan—" he smiled at the detective—"if you'll excuse the presumption." Satan made a "be my guest" gesture with his right hand.

"It wasn't just that night," began Ida. "It began months earlier, when he started getting chummy with Raskalnikov, the Alcott girls, Jo in particular, and then finally Topsy when she started dropping in late every so often. You know there was talk Pharoah and Topsy were tearing it off every now and then. You can't prove it by me. My money was on Jo, but the one time I asked Pharoah about it, he just chucked me under the chin, winked and hummed. He was humming an awful lot that last couple of weeks before he went. He wasn't depressed the way he's been when he first came to work here." She paused, took a sip of beer, scratched her cheek and then continued.

"After all, it was one hell of a comedown for him, ending up tossing drinks behind my bar. I knew he was only marking time here until he could figure out a better scene. Then, two nights before he disappeared, Raskalnikov came in here alone. It was late. Maybe an hour before closing. He sat in the corner of the bar wearing dark glasses and a green beret and that mink-lined astrakhan coat of his, and then when the bar began to thin out a little he waved Pharoah over and said something to him. You know I don't miss a trick around here." Three heads nodded in unison.

"Pharoah just stands there staring at him. I could see his face in the mirror over the bar, and for the first time in months I can see he's scared. Raskalnikov keeps talking, all the time looking over his shoulder out the window like he doesn't want to be caught talking to Pharoah. Then he reaches into his pocket, and Pharoah makes a quick move back like he's expecting him to pull a gun, and I make a quick grab for a bottle. But Raskalnikov pulls out a bill, lays it on the counter and goes. So I ask Pharoah what was up. He just hums. That same damn song. Then he goes to the pay phone near the men's john, dials a number, says something quick into the phone, and hangs up, only now the humming is louder, more cheerful. Same damn song."

"What damn song?" asked Robert.

" 'There'll Be Some Changes Made,' " said Ida. "Then I ask him if he wants to go to the Brasserie for a snack and he says . . ."

❧

"I'm doing my snacking elsewhere tonight, Ida cat."

Ida had a choice of Topsy or Jo and chose Topsy. "That Topsy's bad news, Pharoah."

"Nah, baby" said Pharoah with a quixotic smile, "it depends on how you read her."

"I can't read her as good as I'd like to. She gets blurred. She offering you a job at the Tara Club?"

"Hot damn, Ida cat," he said, patting her cheek, "you got radar the Navy could use."

"When are you leaving?"

"Here? You? I don't rightly know, Ida cat. Is there any rush?"

❦

Ida wiped her moist eyes with the sleeve of her jacket. "And that was that." Her voice was choked with emotion. "The next night he came in as usual, but he kept dropping a lot of things, and he broke a couple of glasses and he looked as though he hadn't had any sleep. But he was cheerful and humming. We didn't say very much to each other. For once, I ran out of words. Like now." She got up abruptly and disappeared into her private quarters.

Robert looked from Peter to Satan. "Any questions?" Both shook their heads No. "Then let's go to the murder."

They spent the better part of an hour rehashing what Peter and Robert had already discussed between them in their apartment earlier that day. They consumed another three rounds of drinks, and Ida remained hidden behind her locked door. Finally Satan stretched his arms wearily.

"The weapon," muttered Robert, "if we could only pinpoint that weapon. A hammer, a poker, a club—something."

"It could help if you could manage to move into that house with your mother and Zoltan. Somewhere in Raskalnikov's room there's got to be a piece of evidence our boys missed. Raskalnikov had the room redone when he moved in, you know. Designed everything himself, from the furniture to the wallpaper. He did it all with that spook of a butler."

"Were you the one who questioned him?" asked Peter.

"Mostly," replied Satan. "I thought they'd get more out of him at the inquest. But, as you know, that was suddenly canceled. I'll say this for him, he couldn't mention Raskalnikov without bursting into tears. Ever see tears drop from somebody's eyes at a sixty-degree angle?" Satan shuddered. "Let's face it. The nut to crack is Topsy Alcott, and how do we reach her? I don't mean by telegram, phone or dropping into her club, I mean how do we reach her vulnerability. And somewhere she is, boys, very, very vulnerable. Other than this, I haven't been much help, have I?"

"On the contrary," demurred Robert, "three heads are better than one. Thrashing this out for the past hour has helped clarify certain fuzzy points, at least in my mind. Take Mr. Raskalnikov's dying word, for example. 'Rosebud.' I was just wondering." He paused for effect. "Might it be a trade name?"

Satan and Peter were no longer tired. It was Satan who spoke first. "I can put a tracer on every Rosebud in the country and see if Raskalnikov or Zoltan was or is in any way connected with it."

"Their connections are not that easily verified," Peter reminded him.

"We can give it a try."

"Then," said Robert, "it would be nice to try

and get to Jo Alcott." He ran his finger around the lip of his glass. "Supposing she *is* in seclusion on one of the upper floors of the club. Mightn't one of us try to get to her?"

"We might," agreed Peter, "we just might. I also suggest the possibility of another chat with Igor."

"That won't be too difficult," said Robert, "once we move into the mansion with Mother. I wish she'd let us know when she and the nabob are arriving."

"I had a *tingling* suspicion we'd *find* you *here!*"

The three heads turned to see Ruthelma and Mr. Rachel bearing down on them.

"And you know when I *tingle* I'm almost *always* right!"

The men got to their feet, Peter and Robert kissed Ruthelma and Mr. Rachel and introduced Satan, and then all five sat.

"*Well!*" she exploded, causing the ornaments on the Christmas tree to tinkle. "Guess whom Rachel and *I* spent an *hour* with *today.*" Silence. "Give *up? Topsy Alcott!*"

Rachel sniffed and signaled Charlotte.

"And *may* I *say,* I think she's *mad, bad,* and dangerous to *know.* Just listen to *this.* . . ."

⌘

The Air France jet from Mexico City circled Kennedy Airport, waiting for the signal to land. In a left-hand window seat in the tourist section, a handsome woman in her late thirties examined her makeup in her handbag mirror for the fifth time.

Still good, she reassured herself. In fact, very very good.

From the corner of her eye she saw a stewardess coming up the aisle.

"Miss!" she called out.

The stewardess fixed a stewardess smile on her stewardess face and in her best stewardess voice, borrowed from a television commercial, asked crisply, "Can I help you?"

"Why are we still circling? We were due to land twenty minutes ago."

"Traffic's a bit heavy tonight. Christmas Eve, you know."

"As in 'Come, All Ye Faithful.' I know. I was just getting a little anxious, that's all."

"First trip to New York?" clip-clip-clipped the stewardess.

"God, no. I used to live here. Been away almost three years."

She turned to the window by way of dismissing the stewardess and looked out at the New York skyline. Almost three years. Three years in Mexico with the man I lured away from his wife and children and Connecticut fireside. Three years with the man who claimed he never had a sick day in his life. Then he eats a taco and drops dead of a heart attack. Then Acapulco, a fitting setting for a bereaved widow with a large haul of insurance.

And Archimedes Zoltan.

Good old Archie. She patted her handbag with its very important letter of introduction. Even now, a year later, she could recall that frail, weirdly pitched voice, like an ocarina being blown by a toothless Croatian.

"Topsy does as Zoltan tells her. When you feel the time is right to form your own publishing company in New York, you go straight to Topsy and she will provide the financing."

Well, she thought, the time ripened sooner than I expected. She looked in the handbag and found the cable, the cable succinctly worded, "Go to New York immediately. Form publishing company. Imperative contact Ruthelma Kross and negotiate new Moulin book. Archie."

New York. Three years. Two dead husbands. Daniel Slater. Seth Piro.

The no-smoking sign above her head lit up, and a brief fantasy caused her to giggle. I should have cabled some of the gang I was coming back. Maybe there'd be a brass band and a huge banner strung across the airfield cosily lettered "Welcome Home, Veronica Urquist."

5

I AM A VEGETABLE. I am a rare vegetable. I am transplanted daily. I am planted in bed at night and in my tub in the morning. I am planted in front of the fireplace and three times a day I am planted at the bridge table, where I am fed breakfast, lunch and dinner. Occasionally when the weather is good I am planted at the window, where I can see out to the garden and across it to Guru's window. I can see portions of the drapes he designed himself with their unique prints that were first offset and then cleverly transferred onto the material, the same process used on his beautifully designed wallpaper. How gifted you were, Guru. You might have been a brilliant artist instead of an aching memory.

I was gifted, too. I could play the piano and the

spinet and the harpsichord and I know the lyrics to over three hundred obscure show tunes. But my fingers are lifeless now. Vegetables don't have fingers. I could sing, and every day, sometimes three and four times a day, I hum my theme song in my mind. 'Happiness Is Just a Thing Called Jo(e).' Funny. I can't sing. I can't speak. All I do is urgle-gurgle.

I have a nurse and her name is Ada Bergheim and though she doesn't know it I strongly suspect she was recommended for the job by the person who knows more about Guru's murder than he'll ever admit. Is he dead, too, I wonder. Why am I still alive? Because I can't talk and I can't write and they're safe as long as I remain a vegetable.

I play a silly game with Nursie every day. I blink my eyes twice when I mean No and once when I mean Yes and she peppers me with questions whenever we're alone, which is often. I think Nursie is nuts. Her brother was that murdered hustler Ben Bentley, whom she admits having loathed, yet she carries a guilt about him. She says her mother's dying words were, "You helped put your brother in his grave." I think she dramatizes everything because she's a spinster and she's lonely. I think she wants recognition. She needs attention. Who doesn't?

Nursie thinks I'll blink her the name of Guru's murderer. She's out of her blinking head. Even if I was sure, even if I'd gotten a look at the face, I'd go cross-eyed before admitting the truth. I'd be as dead as Guru. But I go on blinking. I must have the best-developed eyelid muscles in town. I won-

73

der if Topsy knows there's this portion of my brain that's still alive, alert and aware.

I think Igor suspects. Poor old Igor. They think he's a monster. I know better. He's a dear little man. He's a dear little frightened man. He's afraid to die, because he knows what it is to die. He told me and I didn't shudder. I wept. And Guru wept. *Rosebud*. Why'd he let that reporter get him so drunk? Why didn't he keep his mouth shut? *Rosebud,* my *darling* Rosebud. The jerks. It's right under their noses.

Zoltan's coming back. Zoltan plans to be married. Does she know Zoltan hasn't cut the mustard in thirty years? Does she know how old Zoltan really is? *She* used to get eternal life by bathing in that Haggard flame. Zoltan gets his shot into his veins by Goldberg. Who wants to live forever, anyway?

Do *they* know their days are numbered?

I know who they are. Topsy likes to whisper these little things to me because she thinks she's only talking to herself. Who's Peter and Robert. Satan Stagg. Poor Igor. And poor Ida. They probably know more than they realize. They're no match for Topsy.

I wouldn't be here if I hadn't been greedy. I thought it was the easiest way. Do Meg, Beth and Amy have any regrets? Beth's too dumb. Amy's too naïve. Meg's the one who's not frightened. She's the most like Topsy. Topsy loves her. Topsy says she loves me too. Zoltan says he loves me. Guru said he loved me. Pharoah said he loved me.

And I know their eating habits well. They all

love to eat their vegetables. And I'm a vegetable.

"Come on, sweetheart, open your mouth. Sip this nice Bovril Ada made for you."

Damn! I didn't hear her come in. Did my face give me away? Well, when in doubt:

"*Urgle gurgle.*"

⋘⛤⋙

"That *dreadful* woman. She's *Medea* with all the *snakes* in her *hair.*"

"That was Medusa," said Rachel gently.

"You *mean* there were *two* of them?" Ruthelma's pipe-organ of a voice more than held its own against the onslaught of the din in Ida's Place. Her description of her and Mr. Rachel's meeting with Topsy and its underlying threats had given her center stage for well over half an hour and left her with a terrible thirst and an overpowering hunger.

"You're *sure* you don't want a *bite* of my *pizza?*" There were no takers.

Satan had switched from his pipe to a cigarillo. He was looking past Ruthelma's pizza-crushing jaw at the revelers in the discotheque. He was trying to remember the last time he had enjoyed himself. Robert was making jottings in a small notebook and Peter wished his brother's handwriting weren't so illegible.

"What *are* those hieroglyphics?" asked Peter impatiently.

"A list of suspects, and I've come to the conclusion that you, Satan and I are three of the densest investigators at large. Listen carefully to this."

Robert had their undivided if somewhat annoyed attention. He read off his list of names slowly and with pointed emphasis. "Topsy *Alcott*." He looked up and Peter nudged him to continue. "Next we have *Jo*, then *Meg*, then *Beth*, then *Amy*. I never could remember in which order the four were born to Marmy."

"*Marmy*," said Ruthelma dreamily, oblivious to the rivulet of tomato sauce and olive oil trickling down the sides of her mouth. "She was my *favorite* mother in *fiction* next to Marguerite Oswald."

"Good God!" exclaimed Peter, slapping his forehead much to the annoyance of a fly that had been pecking at his right eyebrow. "*Little Women!*"

Satan burst out laughing. It was the first they had heard his laughter and it was delightfully infectious. Mr. Rachel looked perplexed.

Ruthelma was staring at her husband with mouth agape. "*Little Women*, by Louisa Mae *Alcott*."

Mr. Rachel sniffed. "I don't read paperbacks."

"Fiction," murmured Peter, "pure fiction. Topsy Alcott as in Louisa May Likewise and her four daughters."

"I'm *tingling*."

"And when Ruthelma tingles," said Robert gleefully, "that means we're heading in the right direction. We've got to find out who those four girls really are. Who is Topsy—and what's the mother-daughters act?"

"If it's really an act," added Satan. "Topsy has a wicked little sense of humor."

76

"*Does* she? It *escaped* me. That poor creature *screaming* upstairs. It *sounded* like she was being *tortured*. And that *voice*—that *sound* of Topsy's *voice* when she said, '*Igor*, go to your *room*.' Brrrrr. It's *enough* to make me lose my *appetite*." Ruthelma took a hearty bite of pizza and *mmmmmmmm*'d as she chewed.

Robert leaned toward Satan. "We have to *accept* it as an act. We have to *work* on that premise. It's a possible lead. Think of it if we're right! Topsy and those so-called four daughters are some kind of a front."

"*Part* of a . . ." chomp chomp chomp, "*master* . . ." chomp chomp chomp, "*diabolical* . . ." gulp, "plot."

"Oh, God," groaned Peter. "And now Mother is in the middle of it all. They may be leading the poor lamb to slaughter."

"Now, really, Peter. When was Mother ever a poor lamb?"

"You're right." Peter felt better.

Mr. Rachel suddenly cackled.

"What *is* it, *precious?*"

"Look there. It's too priceless." He was directing their attention to the dance floor. The eighteen-year-old hooker in the mod skirt was dancing a frantic frug. Her partner, who seemed hard put to keep up with her energetic gyrations, was dripping perspiration from the brow of his head, which he held at a sixty-degree angle.

"The *butler!*" gasped Ruthelma.

"Delicious," commented Robert, "absolutely delicious. What say, in the spirit of Christmas, of course, we invite the gentleman to join us for a drink?" He signaled to Charlotte.

❧ॐ❧

Ida stared glassy-eyed at the twenty-five-inch color-television screen. In the past five minutes, she had twisted the selector seven times. A glimpse of Vera-Ellen shouting, "Hey, kids, let's do a show!" gave way to Judy Garland shouting, "Hey, kids, let's do a show!" which led to Gene Kelly shouting, "Hey, kids, let's do a show!," which segued to Toby Wing shouting, "Hey, kids, let's do a show!," which dissolved to Eleanore Whitney shouting, "Hey, kids, let's do a show!," which clicked into Betty Grable shouting, "Hey, kids, let's do a show!," which was switched to Greer Garson's trembling lower lip probably due to no show-business aspirations. Miss Garson was no match for Ida's troubled thoughts.

Maybe I should have told them everything. That threat over the phone may have just been a gag. *Don't talk about Pharoah Love. If you value your life, you'll forget he ever existed.* How do I do that? He's more alive now in my mind than he's ever been. And what's to talk about? What do they think I know that's so dangerous? And who are *they?* What the hell's going on around here, anyway! *If you overheard any conversations between Pharoah and Jo or Raskalnikov or Topsy Alcott, forget them.* Sure I overheard conversations. A snatch here, a snatch there if you'll pardon the expression. Bits and pieces. Small talk. But maybe if you put a lot of small talk together, it begins to add up and it could take on importance. Like what? Like what did I hear?

Son of a bitch. You can't frighten me. You can disguise your voice and sound like Jack La Rue threatening Mary Carlisle, but you can't frighten me. I'm Ida Maruzzi and what I am today I can thank only myself for. I fought and struggled and bled to open this joint and make it the success it is. Damn it. I'm rich. I know everybody who's anybody. I laugh at the mayor's pathetic little jokes. I tell the Mafia to shove off. I even snubbed Truman Capote. So what's to be afraid of?

Damn it! What do they think I might know?

⌘

Robert stared at Igor as he gulped a brandy stinger and sotto-voced to his twin, "I really think he's the ghost of Christmas past."

"Goooddddddd." Igor set his glass on the table and wiped his lips with the sleeve of his jacket. "Igorrrr like stingerssssss."

Ruthelma moved her chair closer to him. "I think your *mistress* mistreats you *mis*erably."

"Igorrrr is useddddd to ittttt."

"Tell me, Igor," said Robert efficiently, "who do you think murdered Guru Raskalnikov?"

"Igorrrr doesss notttt thinkkkk."

"Then Igor knows?" asked Peter.

"Igorrr sayyyy nothinggggg."

Satan put his arm around Igor as he spoke to the others. "Igor's a good guy. He knows how to keep his cool." Igor nodded. "We had a long talk to-

gether at the time of the murder, didn't we Igor?"
Igor nodded. "Igor even wiped the murder room
clean of fingerprints and bloodstains before calling
Mrs. Alcott."

Igor shoved Satan's arm away. "Igorrr no doooo
nothingggg."

"*Igor* needs another *drink*," suggested Ruthelma, gently kicking Rachel under the table. Rachel signaled to Charlotte for refills. Igor leaned
toward Ruthelma.

"Igorrrr likessss youuuuu."

"Oh, *heavens!*" giggled Ruthelma, not missing
Robert's encouraging wink from across the table.
"Another *conquest*." She pinched Igor's cheek.
"Then who *did* wipe up the room?"

"Roommm cleannn when Igorrr finddd
Guruuuuu!"

Robert scribbled swiftly in his notebook, which
he now held out of sight on his lap under the
table. He signaled Ruthelma to keep going and
wished his Christmas gift to her had been more
lavish. She certainly deserved it. But Peter had
convinced him five CARE packages were just the
thing for Ruthelma.

"Well, *then*, what *made* you go to his *room* at
that *hour* of the *morning?*"

"Masterrrr ringggg."

"How *could* he if he was *lying* there with his
skull . . ." she paused to gulp back some rising
pizza, ". . . *crushed*."

"Igorrr oftennnn wonderrrr."

Igor often shrewd, thought Satan, as Charlotte
delivered the fresh round of drinks and pressed just

a little too close to Satan for the detective's comfort. But what the hell, he decided, it's Christmas.

"And *what* about *Rosebud?*"

Oh, F. Lee Bailey, thought Satan, you don't know it but you've met your match in Princess Embonpoint herself.

"Justttt whatttt you readdd innnn *Newsweek.* Guruuuu sayyyy, 'Rosebudddddd' and dieeeee."

"Have you *any* idea who Rosebud *is?*"

The butler moved his chair back. "Igorrr go-o-o-o."

Robert detected the look of fear in his eyes. Robert's eyes darted swiftly to the crush in the remainder of the room, and under the table he gently nudged Peter's knee. Peter's head swiveled slowly.

Topsy Alcott was entering the room with Meg, Amy and an octogenarian gentleman the twins recognized as Sylvester Carp, the munitions king.

Igor grasped the edge of the table and pushed himself to his feet.

"There's no need to be afraid," said Peter evenly. "We're just having a friendly drink." The others at the table were now aware of the presence of the new arrivals.

"Igorrr is nottt afraidddd. Igorrrr . . . sickkkkk." The butler shuffled rapidly toward the men's room.

Robert squeezed Ruthelma's hand. "You did beautifully." When the opportunity presented itself, he wiped some tomato sauce from his fingers.

Two waiters made a flying wedge through the crowded room for Topsy and her party and led them to a table on which there was a card lettered "Reserved." The table was directly across an aisle from the five friends. Topsy espied Mr. Rachel and Ruthelma as she was being seated and smiled in recognition.

"Really, Rachel," she called across the aisle in coyly mock admonition, "you should be at home planning Zoltan's gala."

"My dear," said Mr. Rachel with his haughty sniff, "even Jesus took time out for Christmas."

"I don't believe you've met my daughters, Meg and Amy. Amy, put that doll and that pin back in your purse. And Mr. Sylvester Carp." With a feeble effort, the octogenarian weakly raised a hand in greeting. "Mr. Carp is Amy's fiancé. The pin, Amy, the pin. Put it back." Amy's eyes were smoldering. "Hello, Mr. Stagg," said Topsy. "*Nice* to see you again."

Satan nodded as Topsy focused on the twins.

"Hello, there. Congratulations are in order, aren't they? I'm sure your mother will be *terribly* happy with Zoltan. Say! Why don't we push our tables together and be *really* festive!"

"What a charming idea," said Peter, looking slyly at Robert.

Two minutes later, the tables were pushed together and Meg's raven eyes were devouring Peter. He was aware, but chose to wear a mask of innocence. Sylvester Carp's head rested on his chest, and he appeared to have fallen asleep. No one chose to rouse him.

Topsy addressed the twins. "There'll be an invitation from me in your mailbox Monday morning.

In addition to New Year's Eve, that is. I'm introducing a fascinating new talent at Tara Wednesday night. Perhaps you've seen the teasers in the newspapers."

" 'Ocelot is coming,' " quoted Satan.

Topsy's eyes met his. "That's right. Ocelot. Try to be there, Mr. Stagg. I think you'll find her fascinating. She's Negro too." Satan crushed his cigarillo in the ashtray. Topsy returned to the twins. "I'm so looking forward to meeting your mother. I hear she's *darling*."

"She's priceless," said Peter, and Meg smiled.

In rhythm to the music from the jukebox, Amy was using the table top as a tomtom.

"And your grandmother and your aunt," said Topsy as Charlotte waited patiently to take her order. "Wasn't it Sweet Harriet Dimple they murdered?"

"Only Granny," said Peter with disarming simplicity. "Auntie only helped string up the corpse."

Meg guffawed, and Topsy seized the opportunity to give her order. "A Sazerac on the rocks," she said in a rush. "The same for the girls."

"And for your grandfather?" asked Charlotte with pencil poised.

Topsy glared at him. "You can bring him a pillow if there's one on the premises."

"Sylvester Carp," mused Satan. "Wasn't he one of the backers of the Third Reich?"

"I really don't know," said Topsy. "There's so much apocrypha attributed to the poor darling." She returned to Peter and Robert. "You're such a fascinating family. So talented. Actresses, murderers and writers. You've had an enormous success with *In Cold Water*, haven't you? Tell me, have you selected another subject now that you've decided to abandon the Raskalnikov case?"

Peter opened his mouth to speak, but the tip of Robert's shoe connected with his calf.

"For the nonce we intend to devote ourselves solely to Mother's happiness." Robert smiled sweetly.

"How sweet. Amy, stop that drumming. Two black men at the bar act as though they're getting a message." Amy scowled and folded her arms.

"How long have you known Archimedes Zoltan?" Robert asked Topsy.

"Decades."

"And how long have you known your daughters?"

A small pocket of silence settled over the two tables as the smile on Topsy's face froze. Amy's hand moved to her purse, and Topsy slapped it away.

"Whaht a silly question," said Meg with a smirk.

"You and Amy hardly look like sisters," said Robert.

"I've been ill," said Amy ominously.

"And from the pictures I've seen of Beth and Jo," continued Robert, ignoring Amy, "there's about as much resemblance between them as there is between Dagmar and Perle Mesta. Where is Jo, by the way?"

"Resting." Topsy spit the word like an orange pip.

Peter chose to maneuver into the conversation while Satan listened with a bemused expression and carefully refilled his pipe bowl. "Did you have an affair with Pharoah Love?"

"You're impertinent!" fumed Topsy.

"Part of the family fascination." He turned swiftly to Meg. "Is the pressure of your knee on my knee a warning or an invitation?" Meg's face reddened, and Satan watched Topsy's eyes narrowing over the rim of the glass she held to her mouth. Peter leaned toward Topsy. "I'll bet if we found Pharoah Love he could tell us an awful lot about Raskalnikov's murder."

Topsy's eyes flashed lightning and her words exploded like thunderclaps. "You won't!"

"*Shit*! You mean he's *dead?*"

All heads turned to Ida, who loomed large over Topsy, her approach as swift and as silent as Robert's pencil moving across the pad on his knees.

"Ida dear," said Topsy, "your dress is so becoming. Won't you join us for a Christmas quaff?"

Ida remained standing with clenched fists. "Don't make waves, baby. If I find out Pharoah's dead . . ."

"Yes?"

"Just look out. That's all. Look out." She turned to Peter and Robert. "When you two get a minute, I want to talk to you in private. I'll be at the bar."

"I'm *tingling*."

Mr. Rachel patted Ruthelma's cheek.

"You must do a great deal of reading, Mrs. Alcott," said Peter.

"If you're fishing to find out if I've read your book, the answer is negative."

"I had in mind *Little Women*."

Topsy opened her purse and placed a gold cigarette case on the table. "Of course I've read it," she said, opening the case and extracting a perfumed, silver-tipped cigarette. "And obviously I adored it. Which explains Meg, Beth, Amy and Jo."

"Only superficially," said Satan with a smile.

"Where'd you get the name Satan?" asked Topsy as she lit her cigarette. "I can't imagine your mother having read Dante's *Inferno*."

"My mother was planning on a girl. As I heard it, the girl was to be named after my mother's favorite dress material, satin. She died in childbirth. My father selected 'Satan.' Almost satin, and what he thought of me for killing the woman he adored. He killed himself when I was three months old. So with the help of my Aunt Hattie, I 'jes' growed.'" He added pointedly, "Like Topsy."

Topsy exhaled a puff of smoke. "Give the girl room, boys. She feels crowded in. Anything you want to learn about me is in my official biography. My press agent can supply you with one."

"We've read it, said Robert. "And, like some fiction, it's a classic."

Meg turned to Amy and spoke swiftly. "Are you going to the dance recital with us tomorrow night?"

"No!" snapped Amy. "I can't stand those Fokine ballets."

"Cut the small talk, girls," said Topsy, mustering a modicum of authority. "These gentlemen share a single-minded purpose contrary to an earlier statement that they've abandoned snooping into Guru's unfortunate demise. They are, in four all-too-familiar words, out to get us." She folded her arms and leaned forward on the table. "Gentlemen, when you challenge Topsy Alcott, you challenge the infinite."

Said Robert, "I'm resisting an impulse to kneel and pay homage."

"Write your book," continued Topsy. "Even if it's published, it will be nothing but an amalgam of suppositions, inferences, misstatements and misinformation."

Peter turned to Robert. "She knows Mother." Robert kicked him again under the table.

Topsy turned to Satan. "You've had official word to lay off, yet you appear to enjoy spitting in the eye of authority."

"I come as a friend," said Satan blandly.

Topsy returned to Peter and Robert. "Go ahead. Write the book. If you enjoy wasting time, provoking your betters and endangering the well-being of your mother."

"Careful, Topsy," said Peter, "there are witnesses to that statement."

Ruthelma lifted her head defiantly, and Mr. Rachel wished he had never left Chillicothe.

Topsy sneered. "In my life, witnesses are a figure of speech."

And Amy, purse open, plunged a needle into one of the five dolls she carried.

An agonizing howl was emitted from the men's room.

"Damn," said Amy under her breath, "wrong doll. I'm all thumbs tonight."

Topsy and her daughters stared in astonishment as Igor came shuffling out of the men's room clutching his neck, his face screwed up in pain.

"What are *you* doing here!" stormed Topsy.

Slowly Igor's hand dropped to his side, and Amy snapped her purse shut and reached for her Sazerac.

Satan smiled. "We've been discussing Rosebud."

Topsy's eyes remained fixed on Igor. "Get out of here."

"Igorrr servanttt, nottt slave." He shuffled past the table and was swallowed up in the crowd.

"Rosebud," repeated Peter. "Such a pretty name to be mixed up in such an ugly mess."

Topsy, composure regained, shifted in her seat, put her left arm over the back of her chair, crossed her legs, the silver-tipped cigarette dangling from the corner of her mouth, and briefly reminded Ruthelma of the late Mayo Methot. "Pay no attention to anything Igor says. He's just a stupid, superstitious peasant."

"Topsy!" growled Amy.

"I said *Igor*, dear, not *you*. And you keep your hands out of that purse." Topsy said to the others, "Amy's made a hobby of voodoo. She's sometimes quite good at it. Aren't you, dear?"

"I rarely miss."

"If Igor is such a stupid, superstitious peasant," said Satan, "why don't you get rid of him?"

"It's on my mind."

Robert lowered his glass. "Igor tells us he thinks you cleaned up Raskalnikov's room after the murder and then rang the butler's bell—"

Topsy's fist slammed down on the table top. "Bastard! Igor told you no such thing."

"Well, actually," said Robert with an air of whimsy, "he didn't. But you have to admit it was a good try."

"Amy," said Topsy, fighting to regain control of her voice, "nudge Sylvester awake. I think it's time we were going."

And then Ruthelma gasped. A face and figure she hadn't seen in three years was bearing down on the table.

"Ruthelma! Ruthelma *darling!* And Mr. Rachel! Don't you recognize me? Have I changed all that much? I just flew in from *Mejico!* It's me! Veronica! Veronica Urquist!"

"Oh, Gahhhhhd!" expostulated Meg. "Zoltan's Acapulco doxy!"

"*Veronica!*"

"Oh, Ruthelma *sweetie.* How *good* to see a friendly face. How are you, Rachel? I love your hair that way. Ida didn't notice me come in. She seemed so preoccupied. And what's with the way these waiters are undressed? They carry so little with such pride. May I join you? Marvelous, I'd love to." She pulled a chair from an adjoining table and wedged her way between Ruthelma and

Mr. Rachel. "Waiter! *You!* A double tequila on the rocks, and line the edge of the glass with salt."

Topsy was rising. "Come, girls. It's late."

"Oh, *please* don't go!" squealed Veronica. "At least not until we've met." Topsy sank back into the chair. "I'm Veronica Urquist."

"I'm Topsy Alcott." She announced it like the Second Coming.

"Topsy *Alcott!*" cried Veronica, and Satan expected the room to burst into applause. "But how perfectly marvelous! Do you know what I've got in here?" She was waving her purse under Topsy's nose. Topsy never flinched. "A letter introducing *me* to *you* from Archimedes Zoltan! Well, isn't this a small world! And are these two of your daughters?"

"I'm Meg."

"I'm Amy."

"You're both perfectly gorgeous. You don't look a bit like your mother." Ruthelma nudged Satan. "And who's *this?*" asked Veronica, indicating Sylvester Carp.

"Rip Van Winkle," said Amy dully.

"Ha ha ha!" Veronica suddenly focused on Satan Stagg. "Is it? It looks like him! But it can't be! Pharoah Love! You've changed!"

"I'm not Pharoah Love. I'm Satan Stagg."

"No wonder you've changed. And these two gentlemen?"—smiling vivaciously in the direction of Peter and Robert.

"I am Robert Moulin." A squeal began pushing

90

its way out of Veronica's mouth. "And this is my brother Peter."

"The *Moulin* twins! Oh, this is all too much for me! Topsy and Ruthelma and the Moulin twins! It's like killing so many birds with one stone!"

" 'Killing' isn't a popular word at this table," commented Satan.

"Ruthelma, I have the most fabulous news." Charlotte set her drink on the table, and Veronica brusquely pushed him out of her line of vision. "I'm forming my own publishing company!"

No one heard the alert ringing in Topsy's head.

"With *whose* money?" blurted Ruthelma.

"My own little Santa Claus!" Everyone caught Veronica's unsubtle wink directed at Topsy. "And I may as well tell you right here and now, prepare for one of Veronica's old-fashioned sieges. I intend to begin publishing with the most powerful property I can lay my hands on, and that, Mr. Moulin and *Mr.* Moulin, is the book you intend to write on the murder of Guru Raskalnikov."

"Over *my* dead *body*."

Even Topsy was impressed by the force behind Ruthelma's statement.

Veronica lifted her tequila on the rocks rimmed with salt and blew Ruthelma a kiss.

"If necessary, Ruthelma darling, if necessary."

6

"WHAT GRANDEUR! What majesty! Was it really designed by Stanford White? Look at the symmetry of the marble columns! And that staircase! What Barclay Mill could have done with that staircase and sixty chorus girls! And the tapestries! Oh, Arkie! It's Xanadu! Flora and Fauna will simply plotz when they see this!"

Madeleine Cartier stood in the center of the entrance hall of the Zoltan mansion, swathed in a chinchilla coat lined with ermine (*"Oh, Arkie! Was it really worn by Catherine the Great? No wonder Peter went mad!"*), surrounded by Archimedes Zoltan, one hundred and twenty-seven pieces of luggage, and six footmen lined up against the wall. "Okay, boys!" she shouted exuberantly to the footmen. "One chorus of 'Stouthearted Men' and you can go!"

92

"*Madeleine!*"

The piccolo tweeted in high C. Madeleine froze. ("*In marrying me, Madeleine, you acquire the stature of an empress. Please, please, please learn to behave like an empress!*")

With slow, measured tread Zoltan walked to the head footman. "Why is Mrs. Alcott not here to welcome us?"

"You weren't expected until morning, sir."

"Indeed? Then how do you six come to be here?"

"We've been two days receiving instructions in our duties from Mrs. Alcott and the butler Igor."

"Igor," tweeted Zoltan softly. "Have the luggage taken upstairs and then find Mrs. Alcott and have her come to me at once. The forty-seven cases bound in Moroccan leather you will have placed in my suite. The remainder go to Miss Cartier's rooms."

The footman assigned the task briskly and efficiently as Zoltan slowly crossed back to Madeleine. Her expression was a mixture of bewilderment and petulance.

"Really, Arkie," she said when he reached her side, "now that we're officially engaged, don't you think it's time we shared the same suite of rooms?"

A faint blush tinged his alabaster cheeks as he piped, "That, my dear, would be immoral."

Who do you think you've got here, mused Madeleine, Anne of Green Gables?

"So sorry, darling," said Madeleine, as he took her arm and guided her toward the staircase, "I didn't mean to embarrass you. But I come from Hollywood, where everything's previewed before being given a general release. After you're settled in, come to my rooms and we'll share a bottle of bubbly." She stopped herself from adding, "As appropriately chilled as everything else around here."

"I'm much too weary," he piped. "The journey exhausted me, and it is already three hours past my bedtime."

Madeleine sneaked a glance at her wristwatch. Not yet midnight. My God. He plans lights out by nine! It never occurred to me. He was always off to bed by nine at Goldberg's, but I thought that was *Goldberg's*. But as a steady regimen? Then a fresh thought occurred. Three hours past his bedtime, yet he wishes to see Mrs. Alcott at once. She pigeonholed any comment. He was moving up the stairs slowly and with effort, his right arm tightly clutching at Madeleine's, his left sliding along the marble handrail.

"Arkie, Arkie, Arkie," said Madeleine chidingly, "we could have used the elevator, you know."

"Why?" he tweetled. "Do the stairs exhaust you?"

Madeleine swiftly shifted gears. "Arkie, how soon do you think your friends will spring Fauna and Flora?"

"They will be here before New Year's Eve."

"This year?" asked Madeleine archly.

"I think you are also exhausted," tweetled Zoltan.

94

"Frankly, Arkie, I'm not. I'm going to phone my sons and ask them over."

"At *this* hour?"

"Listen, Arkie, Madeleine Cartier's no twelve-o'clock girl in a nine-o'clock town. I look like Shirley Temple and I *feel* like Shirley Temple. If Bojangles Robinson were still alive, he and I'd be doing a time step up and down this staircase."

"Shirley Temple should be in bed by nine o'clock."

(Oh, God! What am I getting myself into?)

"Now, Arkie, the boys and I will be as quiet as tiny little mice." They reached his rooms, which were directly across from Madeleine's. "Shall I order you some Ovaltine?"

"No, thank you, my dear. Good night." He pecked her lightly on the forehead, slowly entered his rooms and shut the door.

Madeleine exhaled, placed a hand firmly on each hip, and then, lost in thought, sauntered into her suite.

One of the footmen cleared his throat. Madeleine looked up sharply. "Your maids are not expected until tomorrow morning. Would Madame like me to unpack her bags?"

"Madame" said Madeleine acidly, "prefers to do her own unpacking. You can shut the door after you."

The footman bowed stiffly and left. Madeleine studied her sitting room with a professional eye. Lavish. She crossed to the bedroom and entered. Lavish. She crossed to the bathroom and entered.

Lavish. She returned to the bedroom and sat in an easy chair.

Lavish. Lavish and dull. I may have a new face, but it's still the same old me. I need some laughs. I need some excitement. I need some bubbly.

I wonder if this is the room in which Whatsis-name was murdered. It can't be. His was at the back of the house. Must be the one at the far end of the corridor. Stanford White built this house. Arkie refers to him as Stanny. Arkie knew Stanford White? And Evelyn Nesbit? And Harry K. Thaw? But all that was over sixty years ago! Why didn't I start figuring all this out in Switzerland? How the hell old *is* he? Or has he been pulling my leg? And if he has, then pulling my leg is the closest he's come to any part of my anatomy. And Madeleine does not live by bread alone.

She rose, crossed to the telephone on the night table next to the bed, and dialed Peter and Robert's number. On the twelfth ring, the alert answering service answered. They told her where the Moulins could be reached. Ida's Place! Madeleine's dimples twinkled. She hung up the phone, grabbed her purse, gave her face a quick examination in her dressing-table mirror, blew herself a kiss and rushed toward the hall.

◆§§◆

"*Well!*" exploded Ruthelma, puffing up like a beautifully blown piece of bubble gum. "What a *rude* departure!"

Mr. Rachel had been in the men's room, where he had gone to apply a cold towel to his head, and had missed the hasty departure of Topsy and entourage.

Peter explained to Mr. Rachel, "They left in a high dudgeon drawn by six white horses."

"Do you suppose it was anything I said?" asked Veronica innocently.

"You *said* a great *deal*," stilletoed Ruthelma. "Going *on* and *on*"—Ruthelma's wrist was undulating in midair—"and *on* about your *intimate* relationship with Archimedes *Zoltan* in Acapulco as though you were *telling* it to Gerold *Frank*. And going *on* and *on* and *on* about the Raskalnikov *book* when *Topsy's* trying to *crush* it."

"Fiddle dee dee," said Veronica airily, "Zoltan's cable instructed me to tie up the property." She had everyone's undivided attention.

"Indeed?" Peter.

"Really?" Robert.

"Well, now." Satan.

"I kid you not!" She pulled open her purse and waved the cablegram under their noses in turn, then dropped it back in the purse and snapped it shut.

"It's there all right," said Satan, "But I find it awfully hard to believe."

"Why?" challenged Veronica.

"Because Topsy, Zoltan and assorted friends and associates are very much mixed up in the murder. One gets the impression if this murder is ever solved, heads will topple, kingdoms will tumble and a lot of financial empires will go bust."

"But you *saw* the cable. Why would Zoltan tell

97

me to get the book if he didn't want it published? . . ." Her voice trailed away like a dying puff of vapor.

"Veronica," said Robert as he folded his arms and settled back in his chair, "when you seek to close in on something, you close in on all sides. The attempt is being made to corral our talents—" nodding his head toward Robert—"much the same way hunters corner the fox. From one direction, Satan's superiors tell him to drop the case and in no way cooperate with us. From another direction, Topsy threatens us by way of Ruthelma. And from what I strongly suspect is a third direction, Archimedes Zoltan woos and wins my mother, which, believe me, is no trick at all. And my brother and I are more than sure other reinforcements are being drawn up."

For the first time in years, Veronica was wide-eyed. "You make it sound as though they'd think nothing of stooping to murder!"

Ruthelma snorted. "*Raskalnikov* wasn't exactly *tickled* to death! Oh!" And she giggled. "That's almost *funny*."

Veronica sipped her tequila, but tasted nothing. It was as though her taste buds had gone dead. "I've had enough of murder in my lifetime. Ben Bentley. Then Seth."

"And by the *by*. How did Daniel *Slater* go?" Ruthelma asked.

Veronica's look flashed fire. "He ate a taco and keeled over in a restaurant." She turned to Peter and Robert. "I have a suggestion to make." She paused, and Robert gestured her to continue. "Let me tell Zoltan you're giving me the book."

"Is there somewhere in that statement the underlying offer to ally yourself with us?" asked Peter.

"For purely selfish reasons, I have to admit. I want to get my company going. Once I've got Zoltan's backing tied up, the devil can take the hindmost."

"You're putting yourself in a very dangerous position." It was Satan who spoke. "Especially if Zoltan finds out you're double-crossing him."

"Little Veronica can take care of herself." She spoke with the self-assurance of Nathan Hale on the scaffold.

"And how can we be sure you won't double-cross *us*?" asked Robert.

"Very easy. *You* doublecross me. You simply never turn in the manuscript." Her smile was Lucrezia Borgia's after emptying a ring.

Peter, Robert, Satan and Ruthelma exchanged glances. Mr. Rachel stirred his drink with his index finger and sighed.

"Well?" prodded Veronica.

"Under one condition," said Peter, "and I'm assuming I speak for all of us. You convince Zoltan and, through Zoltan, Topsy Alcott, to let our investigation continue unhindered."

Veronica snapped her fingers. "Done."

Robert's eyes twinkled. "You must have given Mr. Zoltan great pleasure in Acapulco."

"Boys—" she leaned forward conspiratorially— "it takes very little doing to give Mr. Zoltan great pleasure. It gives the old goat a sensual kick, if I must say so myself, just having a desirable woman hanging on to his arm. The old boy's impotent."

Robert and Peter yelped as though an electrical switch connected to wires to their chairs had been thrown.

"But he's engaged to marry our mother," cried Robert, "and she can't even *pronounce* 'impotent'!"

"Take it from an old campaigner." Veronica's purse was open and she was unscrewing a lipstick. "In two months not one pass. And when I finally decided to take matters into my own hands, he just tootled in that penny-whistle voice of his, 'But, my dear, that would be immoral.' Anyway, I didn't know it then, but a series of long-distance calls from the formidable Topsy in New York, or so I assume, was already steering our loveboat onto the shoals." She slashed at her mouth with the lipstick and blotted the residue on a napkin. "So it's agreed we're in cahoots?"

All nodded except Mr. Rachel, who was staring transfixed at the entrance to the discotheque. Mr. Rachel was not alone. Everyone else in the room except Mr. Rachel's five preoccupied companions stood or sat staring at the door, frozen in position, as though a wicked witch had passed among them and cast an evil spell. At the bar, Ida clutched a double bourbon, raised it to her lips with some effort and downed it in one gulp without choking.

The chinchilla-clad vision in the doorway, with Shirley Temple curls, Shirley Temple dimples and a winsome Little Miss Marker expression on her face, flung her arms wide like an Olympic champion poised to dive, and gaily caroled, "Hello hello *hello-o-o-o-o-o-o-o!*"

The glass in Peter's right hand slipped and crashed to the floor. Satan grabbed Robert's chair to keep it and Robert from tipping over. Ruthelma clutched Mr. Rachel's paper-thin arm and Veronica gargled, "Who in the hell is *that?*"

"That," sighed Peter, "is Mother."

"Ida darling!" screeched Madeleine. "Don't you recognize me? It's *me!*" She turned to the remainder of the room with a projection that made stereophonic sound seem outdated. "Madeleine Cartier!"

Men and women, teen-agers and senior citizens, drunks and the few that were sober, heterosexuals and their minority opposites applauded, roared, whistled, stomped their feet, and Charlotte wept.

"Darlings! Oh, you marvelous darlings! You remember me! Champagne for everybody! Ida! Oh, Ida darling! You look absolutely divine! You've lost *tons!*" They fell into each other's arms and hugged and kissed, and Ida burst into tears. "Oh, Ida! You make me feel like De Gaulle reentering Paris." Madeleine added as a piquant afterthought, "But all does not glitter that is De Gaulle. Like the new me?"

"Oh, it's just wonderful!" cried Ida between sniffles. "You look just like Shirley Temple."

"That's what I paid for. Now stop that sniffling and take me to my boys." Madeleine grabbed Ida's hand and then saw Peter and Robert coming toward her. "My boys! My boys! My own two baby boys!" She dropped Ida's hand and held out her arms to the twins. "Oh, God! Wait'll you hear what Mother's gotten herself into *this* time!"

Peter reached Madeleine first, embraced her tightly and kissed her. He whispered in her ear, "You look like a song-sheet cover."

"Don't be naughty," she whispered back. "I'll explain everything, with gestures."

Then she clutched Robert to her bosom and kissed him firmly on the cheek. He whispered in her ear, "Isn't this copyright infringement?"

"Well, I *wrote* you they went too far! I plan to have the dimples removed and a cleft put in my chin."

"Then you'll look like Cary Grant!"

"Wouldn't that be *divine!*"

They led her through the admiring throng to their table with Ida paddling behind them like an anxious amah. They introduced Madeleine to Ruthelma and Mr. Rachel, then to Veronica and Satan, and Charlotte came rushing over with a bucket and a bottle of champagne.

"Young man," said Madeleine to the bottom-less Charlotte, "that'll be a silly place to catch cold."

"Oh, Miss Cartier," gushed Charlotte like a gey-ser of charlotte russe, "I've loved you ever since I was a child."

"That was last week, I assume."

"And *where* is your *intended?*" asked Ruthelma perkily.

"Prone in the arms of Morpheus," said Made-leine, removing her pearl-buttoned chamois gloves.

She eyed the occupants of the table warily. "Am I free to speak?"

"You'd say it anyway." It was Robert who spoke so knowledgeably. Charlotte poured a glass of champagne for Madeleine and departed reluctantly at a threatening signal from Ida.

"Mother's done it again. She has leaped before she looked. The old boy is very *definitely* an old boy. My boys, I've had a serious talk with myself in the taxicab, with cunning little suggestions from the hackman himself. Will they ever learn to mind their own business? Anyway . . ." she paused for a sip of champagne, "I am *not* marrying Archimedes Zoltan." She sat back majestically with her arms folded, the expression on her face akin to that of Stan Laurel after besting Oliver Hardy. The expression began to wither under the ensuing pollution of silence. "Well? Aren't you shocked? Dismayed? Annoyed? Say something."

Robert said something. "When do you plan to break the news to him?"

"After he springs Flora and Fauna." To the others, "My mother and sister, for the uninformed."

Mr. Rachel stroked his chin thoughtfully as he spoke. "But there's a big affair being planned for you and Mr. Zoltan at the Tara Club New Year's Eve."

Madeleine brightened. "Oh, I know that! Well, maybe I'll tell him New Year's Day."

"Mr. *Rachel*, my *husband* . . ."

"You're kidding."

". . . is *catering* the affair."

"Oh, well," said Madeleine with a magnificent gesture that almost sent champagne dripping over Veronica's head, "then I'll definitely wait until New Year's Day."

"You may have to wait longer than that," said Robert.

"Whatever the hell for?"

"Mother," said Peter with exaggerated patience, "we have a great deal to tell you. Lean forward and listen."

"I just love this," said Madeleine to Satan, gently squeezing his knee under the table. "It's like a scene out of *The Thirteenth Chair*."

Satan smiled at her politely, and would have regretted it had he known Madeleine's genius for misinterpretation.

"Go ahead, Peter precious. I'm leaning and listening."

7

FIFTEEN MINUTES LATER, Madeleine's ringlets trembled in adjunct to her shock and indignation. Satan's knee trembled in fear of another onslaught from Madeleine's militant fingers, and Mr. Rachel clutched the edge of the table with trembling hands, his heart filled with dread at the realization that everyone at the table might be marked for murder. He had to admire the seemingly cool façade each presented, as though all were patrons of the same mask maker. He had a terrible vision of participating in a mass funeral, but wasn't sure if he'd be there as a mourner or a corpse. He wasn't even sure exactly what threat he, a fashionable caterer, might present to the Topsy-Zoltan axis, other than guilt by association. That didn't bother him too much. He was extremely fond of everyone at the table, save one. He was nursing a growing

hing for Veronica Urquist, and he wished he
could understand why.

Madeleine raised her hand from under the table
to reach for her champagne, and Satan gratefully
seized the opportunity to cross his leg.

"You understand, Mother," said Peter, "why
Zoltan must never suspect you're disenchanted at
the thought of being his empress."

Madeleine enveloped herself in a cloak of righ-
teous indignation. "You don't have to tell me how
to play my part. Of course, I dread the conse-
quences when Flora and Fauna get wind of all this.
The poor darlings. There goes M-G-M and our
comebacks. But one's soul is all the purer for having made sacrifices." She beamed at Satan. "That's
a line from one of my biggest smash hits, *Stick to
Your Knitting*. It was an adaptation from some old
Greek legend or something and I played a gallant
creature named Penelope." She turned to the
twins. "Plan to move in with Zoltan and me tomorrow afternoon. You'll have the room in which
that Guru thing was murdered. As for Topsy Alcott—" she wiggled her nose like Flipper at the
prospect of being thrown a sardine—" I haven't
played a good confrontation scene since that movie
with Helen Vinson." Her face darkened. "I wish
we had some reinforcements. I wish Pharoah Love
was around."

"So do I," said Satan.

"And me," echoed Ida. Her eyes met Robert's.
"The reason I wanted to have a quiet palaver with
you and Peter is that a couple of weeks ago some
shlump voice threatened me over the phone." Mr.

Rachel felt weak. "I was told to stop discussing Pharoah Love and to forget any conversations I might have overheard between him and Raskalnikov, Topsy and Jo. The hell of it is, I've been racking my brain since trying to remember if I *did* hear anything important. But I hear so damn much around here. If there was only some way to unscramble my memory." Her sigh caused a small sirocco in their immediate vicinity.

"I can assign someone to keep an eye on you," said Satan to Ida.

"I can take care of myself," Ida asserted. "I ain't as smart as the rest of you when it comes to this kind of adventure, but this much I can figure out for myself. If they don't want the Raskalnikov case investigated, that means they don't want any other kind of police investigation. And if anything happens to any of us, especially now with Topsy knowing we're all working together, it'll put more life into the case than they want." She added with pride, "No Ida's Place and half of New York is homeless. Of course—" with a shrewdness in her voice Madeleine was to frequently mimic in admiration—"accidents also happen, so let's all be careful crossing streets or shopping at Korvette's."

Veronica had spent the past twenty minutes staring at her fingernails, the palms of her hand, the contents of her purse and occasionally her wristwatch. Her ambivalent nature made it possible for her to listen to the conversation at the table, absorb and disseminate, and lay the groundwork of her own future course of action. Her years of experience as an editor with Saber House, the publishing company her late husband had owned prior to their elopement to Mexico, alerted her to some glaring omissions in the twins' method of investigation. When she spoke, her voice speared their attention.

"To date, how far back have you delved into the origins of the following?" She ticked the names off finger by finger. "Topsy Alcott. Archimedes Zoltan. Guru Raskalnikov. Igor Isogul."

Robert deferred to Peter, who did some finger-ticking of his own.

"One. We know nothing about Topsy prior to her opening the Tara Club three years ago. Her official biography reads like *Alice in Wonderland* as written by Fannie Hurst. Two. Though he's been a celebrated albeit mysterious international figure for well over six decades . . ." (Madeleine gulped more champagne) ". . . a good eighty per cent of what we've read about Archimedes Zoltan reads like speculation and supposition except for an article in *Fortune* some thirty years ago which managed to supply some fairly reliable facts and figures on a proportion of his wealth and subsidiary holdings. As to where he came from and how he got started, there's nothing.

"Three. Guru Raskalnikov. He first appeared on the scene ten years ago. A protégé of Zoltan's, apparently, who traveled on nine passports, making it next to impossible to pinpoint his exact origins. A man presumably possessed of fantastic wealth, but as to how he amassed it, what its disposition was after his murder, we know nothing. We do know he was a ladies' man, thanks to the columnists, but from the seventy-odd ladies we interviewed we could learn very little about him."

"Was he any good in bed?" Madeleine asked out of professional curiosity.

"He must have been," said Peter. Then as an afterthought, "Oh, Mother. Had he only crossed your path, so much of this speculation could have been simplified."

Madeleine's face shone with mother love as Peter continued. "Four. Igor Isogul. We know he's a Transylvanian, was tried and hanged by his country as a traitor thirty years ago, miraculously surviving the stringing, then a twenty-year gap in his history, the threads of which get picked up ten years ago concurrently with the emergence on the scene of Raskalnikov. And let's not forget five, six, seven and eight."

"Meg, Beth, Amy and Jo," contributed Robert.

"And you pose a logical case for suspecting that our five ladies are not blood relations. Let's look at this from the point of view of your book." As she spoke, Veronica leaned on her elbows with her hands propped against her cheeks, looking like a Steichen portrait. "The material to date is not bad, but too slim, even though the suspense works fine. But your eight characters need fleshing out. You've got to know them as well as you made your readers feel you knew the people involved in *In Cold Water*. There you began with Pharoah Love and Seth Piro and then worked backward to Ben Bentley, the first murder victim. Along the way, you picked up everyone else. In other words, one character led to another. Why aren't you doing that *again?* Let's see if I can pencil some character into your blank expressions.

"Forgetting Pharoah for the moment because no one has the faintest lead to his whereabouts, who among your eight protagonists is the most likely to provide the beginning of the link between the members of your unholy octet. Use your head. Igor Isogul. You know he was hanging around Transylvania thirty years ago. Is there a Transylvanian embassy in New York?"

"There most certainly is," contributed Mr. Rachel. "I did a luncheon for them eight months ago. A rather simple affair. Bloody Marys and blood sausages. The ambassador and I are quite good friends."

"Fine. Then you get on the phone to him tomorrow and ask for a tracer on Igor and tell him to keep it under his cloak."

"But *tomorrow* is *Christmas* Day."

"Ruthelma sweetie, Santa takes a back sleigh to the investigation. The boys have got to start moving faster. Whether they're willing to admit it to themselves or not, their mother is enmeshed in an extremely dangerous spider's web. Though her situation certainly doesn't minimize their and everybody else's danger. Four people at this table have been openly threatened. Any day now, Madeleine, Ruthelma, Rachel and I can expect to join that exclusive little club. Igor won't talk? Okay. Get the Transylvanians to talk for him. Veronica has spoken."

The spotlight shifted to Madeleine. "First thing in the morning, in my own inimitable way, I start pumping Arkie on his past, his origins, his relation to the dead man and the Alcott woman."

"But subtly, Mother," warned Robert.

"Subtlety is Mother's middle name. And, boys, once you move into the mansion tomorrow, there are four targets for you to aim at."

"The daughters," said Peter. "Meg was giving me the eye earlier this evening. I, of course, will take immediate advantage of that vulnerability."

"I'd love to get to Jo Alcott," contributed Robert.

"You have your work cut out for you," said Mr. Rachel. "From the altercation we overheard in Topsy's apartment, Ruthelma and I surmise she's in a rather deteriorated state. We overheard the nurse mention some injury to her head."

Satan came to life. "An injury to her head. Guru's skull was crushed, and Jo seems to have suffered an injury to her head. Peter and Robert nurse a theory Raskalnikov may not have been alone in his bedroom when he was attacked. I wonder. I just wonder. Do you suppose Jo has a nickname. Could she be Rosebud?"

"I'm *tingling* again."

Mr. Rachel reached for Ruthelma's hand and held it tightly. He was glad he had married her. He was glad he had come to the decision to rather switch than fight. He even granted Veronica Urquist a soupçon of admiration for having laid out a line of attack for Satan and the twins. But he wished there were less troubled looks on the faces of his companions. He wanted Ida to be her old jovial self. He wanted the weight on his heart to lift. He wanted to shake the terrible premonition that gnawed away at his brain, the premonition that very soon someone, perhaps one of this group, would be the victim of a terribly gruesome tragedy.

❦❦❦

"Stop that pacing, Topsy, and sit down," tweetled Archimedes Zoltan, propped up in the canopy-covered bed. "Everything is going beautifully according to plan."

Topsy came to a halt at the foot of the bed and faced Zoltan with her arms folded. "There's a well-known quotation that begins, 'The best laid plans of mice and men . . .' "

Zoltan's chuckle was like a deflating bagpipe. "I did not attain power and stature by wasting my time constantly fretting. And when faced with errors, I do not weep for them. I amend them. And the murder of Guru was decidedly an error."

Topsy snorted. "You know of a way to bring him back to life?"

"In a sense, my dear Topsy," tweetled Zoltan with a sigh, "Guru is more alive today than he's ever been. More alive than even poor, unfortunate Jo. You're quite convinced her condition is hopeless? There's no chance of her talking?"

"None whatsoever."

"And Pharoah Love."

"There is no longer a Pharoah Love."

"Good. Poor Guru." He shook his head sadly. "That blow was never meant to kill him. Never. Now he's dead, and with him has gone so much information he kept so neatly filed in that brain so cruelly crushed. I really loved him, Topsy. Wherever he is, I hope he forgives me. What a gross piece of miscalculation. Who'd have thought lovely Jo would have been so innocently involved?"

Topsy sat on the edge of the bed and lit a cigarette. "Who'd have thought a lot of things? Who'd have thought the Moulin Twins would come along to write a book on this damned mess? And that detective thing. The Stagg creature. That pale imitation of Pharoah. I'll have to have a talk with the commissioner tomorrow. And what about Madeleine Cartier? Don't you think you went a bit too far where she's concerned? Marriage. Good God. You marry someone like that only when abortions don't take and the woman's honor is at stake. And you're both beyond that kind of involvement. But marriage! Of course it's totally out of the question."

"Totally. Shortly after New Year's Eve, I shall let her down gently. By then, everything I have spent ten years trying to accomplish in this wretched democracy will be completed. You've done brilliantly. Meg, Beth, and Amy have done equally well. Those three idiots they've hypnotized will be fully controlled." His fingers clenched and unclenched like dynamos generating energy for his vocal fervor. His eyes reflected the familiar fanaticism which Topsy always found comforting. "January first, I will have complete control of this country's financial resources. And then—" tweet tweet tweet—"the world shall be mine! Guru—" his voice dropping to a whisper—"so many years of training wasted. I must find another Guru. I must find one soon. I've already overstayed my time."

Topsy listened with a neutral expression, her eyes following the trail of smoke from the tip of her cigarette to the ceiling.

"But I'll hold out until I find another Guru. I wonder if either of those twins is corruptible."

Topsy said nothing.

"No no no." He slammed the quilt three times for emphasis. "I must never grasp at straws. You, Topsy. You can always take over for me should that become necessary."

Yes, thought Topsy, I can take over for you.

"Guru should never have been murdered. What went wrong?"

"I've told you a hundred times. I don't know. Only Pharoah Love knows, and he has disappeared."

"So many loose ends to be tied up before I go. So many people to be eliminated. I must find another Guru. My agents have found a likely prospect in Buenos Aires. A young satyr with a head for figures. There is a similar prospect in Haifa —but will he be able to control the Arabs? So much to do. So little time in which to do it. But first things first, eh, my faithful Topsy?"

Topsy nodded slowly.

"The twins. Madeleine. Satan Stagg. The Ida person. Igor. We must be sure of their silence. New Year's Eve. How I loathe parties. I'm so tired. So tired."

His eyes closed, his head drooped, and a few seconds later he slept. Gently, Topsy arose, stubbed out her cigarette in the ashtray, crossed to the door and left.

She crossed to the door to Madeleine's rooms and pressed her ear to a crack. She heard nothing. Then slowly she turned and stared at the door at the end of the corridor. Guru's door. That room.

"That blow was never meant to kill him. Never. Now he's dead, and with him has gone so much information he kept so neatly filed in that brain so cruelly crushed."

Not really so, Archimedes, Topsy thought to herself as her lips parted in an enigmatic smile. The story I contrived for your ears and your ears only was a brilliant stroke of deception on my part. Guru's murder wasn't accidental. It was deliberate. He needed to be eliminated, contrary to your opinion. He needed to be eliminated because there is another with a desire for power that equals if not surpasses yours, dear darling Archimedes. How old are you now, lover? Ninety-four? Ninety-five? Do I hear ninety-six? Goldberg's injections will soon cease to be effective. There's a limit to how long one can delay the inevitable. And even the inevitable can be hastened. You fought a magnificent battle, Archimedes, and you deserved your spoils. But spoils can dissipate in the hands of a near-senile nonegenarian. Step aside and let youth take over! Step aside gracefully, Archimedes Zoltan, or be *pushed.*

Topsy stood at the doorway to the late Guru Raskalnikov's bedroom.

How often have I unlatched the door to this bedroom?

She unlatched the door and gently pushed it aside.

How often have I stepped over this threshhold, my pulse throbbing, my senses reeling, the sight of you striking my heart like the gong of J. Arthur Rank's trademark? The room befogged with clouds of jasmine incense, my brain befogged by the sight of your magnificent manhood, and the touch of your hand on mine, velvet on velvet. And then your sinewy arms crushing me to your chest, your lips against mine, more velvet on velvet. Foolish Guru, were it not for one fatal mistake, we could still be living on velvet. And after our passion was spent, I would rest my head on your velvet stomach and listen while your velvet tongue regaled my velvet ears with purple tales such as that night you filled my ears with—those delicious if highly improbable anecdotes of the month you spent in Venice with the Chicago sliced-meat heiress. Oh, Guru. And how I laughed at your shaggy-doge stories.

She stood in the center of the room and slowly revolved as though on an invisible mechanical stage. Her eyes drank deeply of the lush Raskalnikov-designed drapes, wallpaper, chairs, sofa, bed and bookcases.

"Guru," she whispered, "Guru, my velvet lover, may your soul burn in hell!"

She flung back her head and began laughing maniacally. Her laughter spread through the room like lava oozing from Vesuvius. It rang and reverberated and bounced and played hopscotch un-

116

til it landed at the feet of the lady in the chinchilla coat standing in the doorway.

"Hello hello *hello-o-o-o-o-o!*"

The laughter strangled in Topsy's throat as she turned and saw Madeleine Cartier, right hand with purse dangling from its wrist poised on the right hip, left hand wielding a half-filled jeroboam of champagne.

Madeleine's voice trilled as it often trilled when she spoke the first line of a new scene. "Don't tell me. Let me guess. You're Topsy Alcott."

Topsy's left hand slowly moved to her ivory throat, and she massaged it gently as she permitted a tiny little smile to intrude upon her face. "You *are* clever, Madeleine. *May* I call you Madeleine? From all I've heard of you, I feel as though we might have been Girl Guides together."

"I've been a girl but only occasionally a guide and by all means call me Madeleine because that's my name." Madeleine took a dozen steps forward, which still left more than one void between her and Topsy. "So this is the room," she said. "So much velvet. Mr. Whatsisname must have been nuts for velvet."

"He designed this room himself." Topsy's voice was dark and throaty. "It's exactly the way it was the night he was killed. Nothing changed. Nothing moved. Nothing added. Beautiful, isn't it?"

"My, yes. Cedric Gibbons couldn't have done better. And what luscious wallpaper. What are those teenchy tiny designs? Hieroglyphics?"

"Guru designed those too."

"What a clever man he must have been. But of course he was! He amassed that amazing fortune, didn't he?" Madeleine turned from the wallpaper to Topsy and decided she preferred the wallpaper to the gray pallor of Topsy's face. "Whatever happened to that vast fortune? Were there heirs? Did it go to charity?" Topsy remained mute. Madeleine, as always, was not at a loss for words. "Yes, I think my boys will be most happy in this room."

Topsy went rigid for a moment, then managed to find her voice. "The boys? In this room?"

"Yes!" Madeleine's voice rang like mingled chimes. "Those two dear old-fashioned darlings insist on chaperoning their mother until she's legally Mrs. Zoltan. Isn't that too cunning of them?"

"Too cunning."

"I'm sure it'll amuse Arkie. Moms and Sis can have the suite on the floor above and we'll all be one big happy family under the same roof at last which has been my dream for years and it's so nice to see dreams come true every so often don't you think?"

Each word acted on Topsy like a bludgeon. Five strangers under this roof with Zoltan. Five dangerous strangers. The Moulin twins in this room. Guru's room. Something's going on.

"Don't you think?" repeated Madeleine.

"Yes, I think."

"And you and I shall be terribly good friends, won't we! How's about cementing that with a few drops of vintage bubbly?" She waved the champagne in Topsy's face.

"It's a bit late for me, I'm afraid. I'm rather tired." Topsy moved toward the door.

"Oh, don't go yet! I'm not the least bit sleepy! And, heavens, do you realize? It's Christmas! I must remember to hang up a nylon. There must be tumblers in the bathroom—"

"I have to be going." Topsy's words formed an effective barrier, and Madeleine moved away from the bathroom.

"Of course," said Madeleine with her patented smile, "if you insist. We can talk again tomorrow. It'll be so cozy being neighbors. In and out of each other's houses just like girls next door."

"Good night, Madeleine."

"I'll see you out."

"Don't bother. I know my way."

"Of course you do. Good night. Oh, Topsy . . ." Topsy halted in the doorway. "Merry Christmas!"

"Merry Christmas," and she left.

Madeleine crossed to the door and watched Topsy disappear down the staircase. Swiftly, Madeleine rushed to her rooms, shut the door and crossed to the phone. It was an effort to keep her finger from shaking as she dialed.

On the fourth ring, Peter's sleepy voice inquired, "Yes?"

"Peter? It's Mother! Blow the cobwebs out of your head and hear this. The second Mrs. de Winter just had her first encounter with Mrs. Danvers!"

Peter nudged Robert awake, mouthed the word

"Mother" as he pointed to the phone, and then placed the phone between them. Hungrily they assimilated every word of Madeleine's meeting with Topsy in the Guru bedroom.

"Good old Moms," commented Robert into the phone.

"But the laughter, my dears. You should have heard the laughter! Gale Sondergaard in *Anthony Adverse!*"

"You have to admit," said Peter tauntingly, "she's quite an alluring piece?"

"Peter," said Madeleine, her voice dripping icicles, "she couldn't lure a man off a burning ship. But, my dears, when I casually let it drop you were moving into the death room . . ."

Death room.

"Mother? Mother! Are you there?"

"I'm here, all right. I just paused to shiver. Someone must have walked over my grave."

❧

With a sob, Igor Isogul threw back the comforter on his bed, switched on the night light, shuffled to the statue of the Virgin Mary cradling Christ in her arms, knelt and prayed.

"Maryyyyy, Jesusssss, thissss issss Igorrrr. Igorrrr. Igorrrr needssss yourrrr comfortttt. Igorrrr needssss protectionnnn. Igorrrr sayyyy Igorrr nottt frighteneddddd. Igorrrr lieeeeee. Igorrrrr frighteneddddd shitlesssss. Helppp Igorrrr . . . or soonnn . . . Igorrrr dieeeee!"

He scrambled to his feet in a sudden panic, tried the door, tested the five bolts and two chains installed by him the day he took up residence in Topsy's ménage, then shuffled to the windows and reassured himself they too were tightly secured. Then he whispered across the room to the statue.

"Igorrrr dreammmm of deathhhh. Olddddd Transylvaniannnn superstitionnnn. Dreammmmm of deathththth meannn deathththth nearrr. Igorrrr veryyyyy superstitioussssss."

He shuffled back to the bed, switched off the night light, crawled under the comforter and hid his head under the pillow. But sleep eluded him. There was a decision to be made. The look on Topsy's face in Ida's Place had convinced him of that. On top of the incident in Jo's bedroom, he was finally convinced Igor was unpopular. There must be someone to go to. Someone to confide in and then give him protection.

Maybe three someones. Just maybe.

☙§§❧

The red Jaguar speeding along the New Jersey Turnpike toward New York clocked eighty-five miles on the speedometer. Ocelot wore a leopard-skin coat over her lynx slack suit, and her traveling mask. Her hands, sheathed in lynx-taloned gloves, gripped the steering wheel firmly and with assurance. The smile on her face reflecting in the windshield was more minx than lynx.

Yes, Ethel, she thought to herself for the twentieth time in the past hour, when you've planted your garden and watered it and mulched it with loving care, everything's coming up roses. *Ocelot is coming!* Coming, hell! Ocelot's *here!*

All the black power in the world is centered in the core of this cat lady. And, world, you better believe it. All my eggs are in one basket, and lettered on that basket is one indelible name: Topsy Alcott.

The look on that cop's face when I drove through the toll station. Halloween my ass, Buster. This ain't no masquerade. This is reality! This is *Ocelot*. The first. The last. The only. A true original. And I am the most!

She souped the car up to a hundred and then hummed and hummed and hummed.

8

It was the tired hour at Ida's Place, when levity was as forced as a politician's promises. It was the hour when faces took on a look of pained desperation, when alcohol-laced laughter was like the fading echoes of ambulance sirens, when friendly persuasions gave way to threatening entreaties. It was the hour that added weight to Ida's too-heavy heart, when she could have dueted with most of the familiar phrases that began boomeranging around the room as the hands of the clock neared four and closing time.

"Would you like to come to my place?"

"Do you live alone?"

"I thought we might go to my place for a nightcap."

"You've had enough!"

"My wife understands me, which is why she's home and I'm here."

"Yes, you do remind me of my mother. She's also dead."

"I don't do that sort of thing."

The bartender began checking the cash receipts, the waiters began clearing the tables, and Ida cleared her throat.

The pipe in Satan's mouth was as cold as his five fingers embracing the freshened glass of seven and seven, almost as cold as the optimism which had turned his troubled mind into an open hearth several hours earlier.

"Trust the twins," said Ida, shrewdly reading his mind.

Satan placed his elbows on the bar and propped his chin on his fists. "I have to trust them." The words stepped gingerly around the stem of the pipe clamped between his teeth. "I've gone beyond the pale. I'm committed but I'm worried, to which I'm entitled." He took the pipe out of his mouth, placed it on the bar, and with one hand massaged the back of his neck. "The wheel's spinning and I've placed all my chips on number two. The odds are rotten but I've a gambler's instincts. I've placed bets before, but never a stake as high as this one. Ida lady, I just might find myself back pounding a beat if we don't come up with the right answers. Maybe worse. And that'll make two of us black brethren who have beclouded our so-called smog-free police department. To quote David Susskind when confronted by his intellectual superiors, 'Woe is me.'"

Ida shifted on the bar stool, her left ear tuned in to Satan, her right ear tuned in to the residue of barflies, both eyes x-raying the bartender as he checked the cash register.

"When you can't find a hero in yourself, you make do with a reasonable substitute. So Pharoah Love became my moon and I his satellite. Moon's gone and satellite's sputtering. I hold a master's degree and almost no degree of mastery. And on my job, I'm beginning to feel persecuted and that is the beginning of the end. I sat at that table for over three hours and listened to a lot of shrewdness, and felt very, very inadequate. Dammit." He slammed a fist on the bar. "I couldn't contribute a damn thing because, dammit, I've gone dry on this case and all out of fear. Afraid for my job. Afraid of the higher-ups." His voice lowered three octaves. "Afraid of Topsy Alcott."

Ida's eyes dollied into Satan's. "She's more afraid than you are, baby. I know women, kid. If I know anything, I know women. She's afraid. That's why I ain't afraid." She pointed an index finger at Satan's nose. "You listen to me. All the time the gang of us sat together at those two tables, I almost never took my eyes off her. That broad knows you guys are closing in on her and she don't quite know how to handle it. It's coming at her from all directions. There's the twins, there's Madeleine, there's Veronica and there's *you*. One at a time she can handle. You keep chipping away at her, kid, and she'll begin making some wrong moves. I know the type. She thinks she's got it made. She thinks she can outfox everybody. She thinks she's got everything going for her. Inside she knows better. I know. I've played the scene myself."

Satan stared into his drink and nodded slowly as Ida spoke, wanting hungrily to throw his arms around her, not for passion but for gratitude. But demonstrative gestures didn't come easily to a man who saw his walk through life as a hike on a path of eggshells. He simply continued nodding, admiring the authority in her voice and the courage in its timbre.

"Let me tell you something, baby, and you take it from Ida Maruzzi—" the twenty-one-gun salutes in her eyes hypnotizing the detective—"there's gonna be a lot of fast action soon. And in fast action there's slipups. I saw Seth and Pharoah and that rotten Ben Bentley making their mistakes. Overconfidence. The world on a string. Strings fray when they're overloaded. This broad's overloaded. Go home, take some bromo, say your prayers and include a kind word for yours truly, and then get up in the morning and start tracing that goddamned Rosebud." She scratched her cheek and refocused on the bartender. "Ten to one it's a stripper." Her eyes narrowed into slits. "Hey, mucilage fingers." The bartender quivered. "That ten-spot belongs in the money sack, not your pants pocket." Green moved swiftly from pants to bag.

Satan raised his glass to Ida. "Merry Christmas, baby."

"Some Christmas," muttered Ida. Then she roused herself and bellowed, "Last call!"

"Holy absinthe!"

Ida's knee nudged Satan's as she whispered, "Beth Alcott."

Satan turned to the doorway. She looked like cotton candy that was beginning to melt. Her mink coat hung loosely from her shoulders, her hair hung loosely dissheveled, her eyes hung loosely unsocketed, and she was loosely smiling.

"Hello, Beth baby!" boomed Ida jovially as she crossed to the entrance. "Come on over and have a Christmas drink. You too, pal."

Beth's escort was a cabdriver. Beth tugged at his leather jacket and pulled him to the bar.

"I want a Sazerac." Oliver Twist asking for his second bowl of gruel couldn't have sounded more plaintive. "I just got thrown out of Cheetah." She turned to the bartender, screwing up her face like Jackie Cooper in *Skippy* on being told his dog had been hit by a car. "I want a *Sazerac*."

"A Sazerac," repeated Ida, with a quick wink that telegraphed the message "Make it strong." Then she asked the cabdriver, "What are you having?"

"My fare," he said with a trace of Queens Boulevard.

Beth smiled beguilingly. "I was supposed to meet Topsy here. I was having dinner at Elmo's with my financey . . ." Satan cringed ". . . but he started having one of his heart palpitations or something and they hadn't even brought the check. So somebody said get him to a hospital so I took him to Cheetah's and deposited him in the coatroom but when I went to claim him he was gone or something and boy oh boy oh boy Topsy won't like that at all. So I made such a fuss they eighty-sixed me and I found Homer here—" squeezing the cabdriver's arm—"and I thought maybe I'd still find Topsy here because it's only a little after midnight."

"It's almost four A.M." said Ida.

Beth tossed her head as she tried balancing on a stool. "Time has no meaning."

Ida passed a knowing look to Satan, paid the cabdriver, who left muttering a Homeric oath, then sat next to Beth, who clutched the Sazerac glass with both hands, lowered her head and shlurped. Satan replaced the cold pipe with a warm cigarillo, then moved his head toward Beth's ear.

"Remember me?" he inquired with just the right suggestive note.

Beth adjusted her focus and then smiled. "I never forget fuzz." She tried straightening up. "My daddy always said, 'Peanuts sweetheart . . .'" she hiccuped, smiled vaguely, and then finished the sentence, "'never forget fuzz.'"

"Where's Daddy now?" asked Satan softly.

"Who gives a damn?" she started to fall forward. Ida put her arm around her waist and propped her back up. "He was no damn good anyway. Always beating up on us." Satan was positive the room was reverberating with his heartbeats. Ida held the Sazerac glass to Beth's mouth, and a tiny red tongue darted out like a chameleon's and lapped away for a few seconds. "Boy oh boy oh boy. Topsy ain't gonna like none of this. Oh boy oh boy she ain't."

Satan put his arm around Beth's shoulder. "Your daddy beat up much on Topsy?"

"Ha ha ha ha ha!" she slapped the edge of the bar as she shook Satan's arm loose. "That'd be the day. Why, if Topsy'd known him—" She caught herself. "That's a damn good Sazerac. Real damn good." She hiccuped again, fell into a drunken silence, and then just as quickly roused herself. "Sazerac's for ladies. That's why Topsy taught us to drink 'em. I'm a Nooooo Orleans debutramp, 'cept I can't do that nigger accent." She winced and looked at Satan shyly. "Oops."

Satan managed a friendly smile. "You can't kid me. You're not from the South."

"Who the hell wants to be?" She dipped a finger into the Sazerac and then licked it. "Are you bored?" The question was directed to Ida.

"To tears."

"I'm bored. Tired of this sitting around. Tired of old Jonah." Old Jonah, thought Satan. Jonah Richards. Airlines. Shipping lines. Banks. "You know," she said to Ida, "a girl likes to get laid every so often. I feel like a frigging nun."

Satan laid his hand on her knee. "Would you like to come home with me, baby?"

"And *then* what?" the voice came from behind them.

Meg and Amy each grabbed an arm and pulled Beth from the stool.

"I liked that," said Beth through a hazy grin. "Let's do it again."

"Get her to the car." Amy obeyed the order promptly.

"Car?" said Satan mockingly. "Not 'cah'?"

"Mr. Stahgg," said Meg, her voice as raven as her hair, "you just soon might see the fulfillment of your death wish." She pivoted toward the door and left.

Ida and Satan looked out the window and saw Amy push Beth into the front seat of a Volks, get in next to her and shut the door as from the other side Meg got in behind the wheel, slammed the door shut with Amazonian force and drove off.

"Like I said," said Ida, "keep chipping away and they start making wrong moves."

Satan raised his glass. "Merry Christmas."

❧৪৫৯

"What did you tell them?" shouted Amy, shaking Beth mercilessly. "What did you tell them?"

Beth turned slowly to Amy, opened her mouth, and threw up.

❧৪৫৯

The logs in the fireplace of Topsy's bedroom blazed, crackled and popped. Topsy stood with one hand on the mantel piece, the other propped on her hip, staring down at the figure curled up on the rug, smoking a cigarette and grinning kittenishly.

"Topsy a bit turvy," purred Ocelot.

"Topsy damned worried." She moved away from the fireplace to a sideboard and poured herself a brandy. "Zoltan I can handle. Igor I can handle." Her voice rose with each statement. "Men I can handle. But *those* three!"

"What three?" inquired Ocelot disdainfully.

The blaze in Topsy's eyes matched the blaze in the fireplace. "The Ritz Brothers. Who the hell do you think I mean? The Moulin twins and Stagg."

"Have tuxedos," sighed Ocelot, "will travel."

"Have a little too much for comfort," said Topsy grimly as she sank into a chair. "The Moulin twins alone, Stagg alone, that I can handle. But together in one pot along with old hello-hello-hello-o-o-o, the Urquist thing and the others, that's a pretty spicy *pot-au-feu*. We have to make a move, and soon."

"Like what?" Ocelot turned over and stretched out on her stomach facing Topsy. "They're not going to find out anything. Who dares talk?"

"Igor." Topsy blew the name in Ocelot's face like a poisoned dart. "Christ! Why the hell'd Jo have to be there?"

"As you have frequently said, Topsy, the best-laid plans etcetera etcetera etcetera." Ocelot sat up, en route marrying her cigarette to the blazing logs. "Well, nothing's stopping Ocelot! *My* timetable's going according to schedule and there'll be no last-minute changes. As for Igor beaver—" her fingers curled and uncurled—"I'll have a little talk with him."

"There's still Zoltan. As long as there's Zoltan . . ."

"We don't dare."

"Why not?"

"Are you mad?"

"I have lately wondered."

Ocelot sprang to her feet and crossed to a window, staring out at the silent street. "He's old.

He's very, very old. And you have to make a move before he creates another Guru. It's got to be soon. You know it's got to be soon." She turned to Topsy. "You've already got your fingers on practically all of it. You've had the route to South America set up for months. We lay low there until the heat's off, and then," she said with a knowing smile, "we come back and complete the takeover." She advanced slowly. "Zoltan only has you now. You're the last link."

"What about the girls? What about Jo? Poor Jo."

"Poor Jo. Poor girls. Poor everybody. Except us."

Topsy took her hand and kissed the palm. "Except us." She looked up and saw two fiery cat's eyes. "Calm down, sweetheart. Topsy knows how to cope. It's just a matter of slowing down the opposition until it's time for the final move."

"Ocelot's an old hand at faulty brakes."

They heard the Volks pull up outside with an agonizing screech. Both went to the window swiftly and looked out. They saw Amy and Meg dragging Beth from the front seat, and then Meg looked up and saw them at the window. Topsy cursed and rushed toward the hall.

❧

The bleak morning light seeped through the drapes, and Zoltan stirred. His skin was too tight and his bones too brittle, as they always were at this hour of the morning. He had barely slept and felt irritable. With an effort he propped himself up against the pillow, reached for the glass of water on his night table and took some. Then he leaned back and tried to assort his thoughts. The body may be old, but the brain is still alert and nimble.

I am old, Father William, I am old.

Topsy. Guru. Jo. Igor. Madeleine. Peter. Robert.

Oh, please, please. Line up and wait your turn. He sought mathesis and found it. Discipline the mind to obey as you have disciplined countless millions to obey.

Begin with Madeleine.

Gino did his job well, jockeying Madeleine to Goldberg's. Why did I so stupidly propose marriage? She could have been easily strung along until the book on Guru was eliminated. It all looked so good on paper. So simple. Hello hellooo hello-o-o-o-o. He chuckled. Quixotic Madeleine. Ephemeral Madeleine. Gossamer Madeleine. Clever Madeleine. Comparing me to Aethe, Agamemnon's stately-maned steed. Where did she look it up? Had she been reading Mary Renault? And the nonsense of purchasing a movie studio for her. The nonsense of releasing her mother and sister from prison. What made me think I was in love with her? It was the day they removed the bandages. What love have I ever had in my lonely life? What deep emotion have I ever felt in ninety-seven years? Once on both counts. The evening I sat alone in my Carpathian castle and ran a movie on my sixteen-millimeter projector. And a tiny sprite sang "Animal Crackers in My Soup" and won my heart forever.

Shirley Temple.

And they removed Madeleine's bandages, and little Shirley was reborn. Only my little Shirley is in truth big Madeleine, and it is foolish to try and recapture the past. I shall let her down easily.

Now Topsy.

He took another sip of water and with trembling hand replaced the glass on the night table.

Topsy has changed since Guru's murder. This is not the Topsy I knew twenty years ago. Her variety of sinister expressions in our brief verbal intercourse last night. I have seen them before. Where? He prodded his memory. Lizzie Borden. That party in Boston at Nance O'Neill's. Lizzie discussing the family maid who had given damaging testimony against her. "That shanty-Irish dyke!" Lizzie cried. The memory of another sinister expression comes to mind, and that shrill, miserable voice. "What the hell do you mean do I have change for a quarter? Whaddaya think I am, a streetcar conductor?" Hetty Green. And to think of the stock-market tips I gave her. "Stop frowning and give Ella a hug." Jameson Hurst. Sad, ridiculous, ambivalent Jameson Hurst. How beautifully you served me in organizing the world's underground homosexuals. No one knew that was the source of your wealth, or will ever know. Your secrets died with you and your doppelganger Ella. And that absurd funeral, in, of all places, Philharmonic Hall.

But they are dead and Topsy lives and I see her ambition growing and broadening and taking on the size of an uncontrollable mutant. And you are a mutation, Topsy. I constructed you as Frankenstein constructed his monster. The monster destroyed Frankenstein.

Do you plan to destroy me, Topsy?

Do you think I believe the story you so artfully constructed explaining Guru's *accidental* murder?

You are making one serious error. In overestimating yourself, you underestimate me. But I give you this. You are shrewd, perceptive, brilliantly calculating. You can see beneath layers of skin. You perform an autopsy without making an incision. You are everything I taught you to be. Does the student again plan to serve the teacher hemlock?

Does it matter any longer?

Why do I continue to permit myself to be driven by this compulsion? What did Sigmund tell me at one point in those three months I permitted him to treat me in Vienna? "Your mother deprived you of her nipple." Is the world my nipple? I can't even remember my mother, so why bother? Why don't I give it all up and retire to Florida? I can't. I'm not Jewish.

Oh, yes. Veronica Urquist.

Does my shrewd, calculating Topsy suspect? Does she really have an idea why I cabled Veronica to secure the rights to the book? Does she know that I have had time to think, those weeks at Goldberg's? I want the book written. I want the facts on paper.

It is a weapon. A weapon against perfidy. You tell me Igor murdered Guru in a fit of hysterical anger. You tell it so well. So convincingly. Guru was arranging to return Igor to Transylvania. Igor was beginning to pose a serious threat. If so, my impeccable Topsy, why do you harbor Igor under your roof?

Poor Igor. When I think of your name, the room darkens.

"Hello hello hellooooo! Open your eyes and drink your fill of me! It's merry merry merry merry *Christmas!*"

Zoltan turned his head slightly and mustered a smile.

"I did not hear the door open."

Madeleine crossed the room, drew open the drapes and then crossed to the bed and bounced atop it next to Zoltan.

"I have the most delicious news for you! Guess who's moving in *today!*"

Zoltan closed his eyes and waited.

"The *twins!* They insist on acting as our *chaperons!*" She stretched out alongside him and snuggled close. "Aren't they delicious?"

Thor, pleaded Zoltan, send a thunderbolt.

⊷§§⊷

Amy carefully dusted the row of dolls on the shelf above her bed. Each had a tag clipped to it. There was one for Madame Nhu and one for George Rockwell (Amy wasn't sure what he was up to, but she didn't like his face) and one for Barry Goldwater (she had removed the two pins after the election returns were in) and three for a trio of agents at Ashley-Famous who had told her she had no future as an exotic dancer. There were dolls that represented the twins and Madeleine and Igor and even one for herself when she felt the masochistic urge for self-punishment.

"Will you put down that damned rag and pay attention to me?"

Meg sat at Amy's dressing table brushing her hair in a furious flurry of activity. Amy sat down on the bed cuddling her Sandy Koufax doll and with a wicked grin stroked one of its shoulders tenderly.

"God knows what Beth might hahve spilled at Idah's lahst night." Then Meg shuddered. "But the way Topsy beat her. Oh, Gahd, Amy. The look on Topsy's face. The ahful things she said. I mean she's ahlways been kind to us, but lately hahven't you noticed the ahful change that's come over her? I'm beginning to think maybe we're not safe any lahnger. We ought to start thinking for ourselves! Amy! Are you paying attention?"

"I'm way ahead of you."

The hand holding the brush froze and Meg's raven eyes found Amy. The lids half hid the almond eyes.

"I've been pumping Igor. And let me tell you, when you pump hard at that well it turns into a gusher. There's more behind this caper than you, me and Beth marrying those alte cockers. Okay. That's what we've been getting paid for. But you know me, kid. I like to learn new things. Like you ever heard the word 'cartel'?"

Meg shook her head No.

"It means takeover, baby. And that's what I think is behind all this. A takeover. And you know what cartels do once they take over? They get rid of excess baggage. I'm glad you admit you're worried. I been afraid to say anything because you and Topsy have been so thick."

"Only since Jo got sick."

"Sick me eye. She got her bean bashed." Meg's eyes widened. "The night Raskalnikov got the kiss-off. Guru told me. He didn't see for sure. But remember Raskalnikov's last word. 'Rosebud.' You know what that means."

"I've known all along. I've suspected Jo knows more than she's able to tell."

"She's lucky she can't talk. Otherwise, I think she'd've been dead a long time ago."

"Jo?" Meg placed the brush on the dressing table. "Topsy would never let that happen. Not to Jo. She was her first. She was more a daughter to Topsy than any of us. But still . . ."

"Right. You know Topsy's motto: 'All for one and I'm the one.' She could never get Zoltan to marry her, so she had to find another way to lay her hands on his empire." Amy winked. "You gotta keep your eyes open and your ears to key-holes, baby. Remember the smart cooky that brought me up, baby, and taught me everything I know. Zelma the Zombie. Let me tell you, baby, Zelma's got pins that can start earthquakes. Remember that blackout we had here a couple of years ago?" Meg nodded and Amy's face bristled with pride. "Zelma." She shoved the doll aside. "That'll teach Lindsay to snub her when he was stumping in Harlem. When I told Zelma I was going in on this deal, she got out the old ear of eft and eye of newt, cooked up a little jambalaya and told me to watch my step." She thumped her chest with a thumb. "This kid watches her step. She knows there's trouble brewing. The twins. Satan Stagg. That Veronica bitch. That caterer and his sloppy sidekick. And this one." She reached up and took down a doll. "I made it this morning."

Meg gasped. "*Ocelot.*"

"I ain't Pearl Harbor, baby. Nobody catches *me* napping."

∾ॐॐ∾

Peter sent a kiss wafting into the mouthpiece of the telephone. The kiss traveled swiftly and emerged at the other end, where it settled in Madeleine's contented ear. She hung up the phone and did a time step to the bedroom, where a steaming tub awaited her, en route singing at the top of her lungs, "Let's all stick together, together we don't fall apart."

Robert looked up from the notebook in which he had scribbled the previous evening at Ida's and caught the I-ate-the-mouse expression on Peter's face.

"Our room at the Zoltan mansion is being prepared for us," said Peter triumphantly.

"Good old Madeleine," responded Robert, the beam on his face strong enough to light up Grauman's Chinese. "What else did she say?"

"It seems there's been a bit of a to-do at Topsy's involving Beth."

"Ah?"

"Ah. Mother was there when Zoltan took a call from Topsy. And apparently Zoltan seems genuinely anxious for us to write the book."

"Well, well, well. Allah is good."

"But Mother doesn't trust it."

"Allah is bad. Her intuitions can match Ruth-elma's tingles any day."

"He's also stalling about springing Flora and Fauna."

Robert smiled maliciously. "I might even force myself to learn to call him Daddy."

Peter poured himself a cup of coffee, buttered a piece of cinnamon toast, and drew his chair closer to the breakfast table at which both were seated. "It also seems that the Ocelot creature is now a house guest of Topsy's. Apparently arrived some-time during the night."

"On all fours?" Robert closed the notebook and dropped his pen on the table. "House guest. Is it usual for club owners to house their talent under the same roof?"

"Only if they're having an affair. Whoops, what a naughty thought. Topsy strikes me as unnatural, but not *that* unnatural."

"Yes, let's scratch that thought for the moment. You put it between covers and it makes the critics' hackles rise. But still, this Ocelot-Topsy alliance just might provide a bit of sustenance for the rigid diet we've been suffering, what with the lack of vitamins we call leads."

"Oh, we're beginning to get leads. Lots of nice fat, juicy little leads. From Guru. From Ida. From Satan Stagg. Even from Topsy herself. But what we really need is one good break."

Peter was about to take another bit of toast

when the phone rang. Robert rose and answered it.

"Good morning, Satan," he said cheerfully. Then he listened. His eyes lit up. His hair suddenly glowed with a healthier sheen. His cheeks turned rosy, and then he said into the phone, "Wait a minute. I want Peter to hear this too. Peter. Quickly. Get on the extension. Satan had a run-in with Beth Alcott, Meg and Amy at Ida's after we left."

Peter leaped from his chair and dashed toward the bedroom extension.

❧⸙❧

Beth groaned. Her face was damp with tears. Her body ached in a dozen different places and she felt too weak to examine the welts and bruises. What's a nice kid like me doing in a mess like this? What the hell did I say to that spook fuzz at Ida's last night, anyway? When was I at Ida's? How did I get there? Where'd I lose Jonah? Jonah. Ugh.

That look on Topsy's face last night. Holy cat o' nine-tails! She almost murdered me. Beth rolled over on her back and stared at the ceiling. Murder. She almost murdered me. And neither Amy nor Meg made a move to stop her. And that spooky bitch in the cat's mask. So that's Ocelot. Evil bitch. I know bitches and I know evil. I've been surrounded by both for three years. It sounded like a nice, cozy deal when I agreed to it three years ago, but since last Christmas Eve, when poor old

Rasky-wasky got his, things ain't been the same around here. Meg's gotten mean and touchy, Amy's going round the bend with those dolls and those pins, Topsy's started talking to herself, Igor's sending everybody up the wall and Jo's about as useful as a television ingenue. Meg and Amy know how to look after themselves. Meg's got her black Irish temper. I still believe in Peter Pan and applaud for Tinker Bell. Amy can stick pins in her dolls. But I can't do that. Some of my best friends were dolls.

What happens to me now?

I ain't waiting around to find out.

What did Poppa always say before they gunned him down during that filling-station heist? "When you ain't sure, baby, head for the border." I wonder which direction's Canada. They say it's cold up there. Then it must be north. That's what I'll do. I'll grab the Volks and make for Canada. I'll collect my bonus and go. She sat up and bit the palm of her hand to keep from screaming out in agony.

Holy osteopath! Are my bones broken? I don't think so. When do I dare go? I've got my jewels and some cash hidden in the bottom of my trunk. I'll dye my hair and wear dark glasses. And if they don't lay off, I'll go to the Mounted Police and spill all. What the hell. I got paid to take orders. Ain't that what all them German war criminals claimed?

Nobody's gonna marry nobody around here, anyway. We've drained our Johns of all the information Topsy wanted. She knows where all the bodies are buried. I wonder if she ever passed the stuff on to Zoltan. I know she's bought heavily into Jonah and Sylvester and that goon Texan of Meg's who knows more then he ought to know about a lot of things that have gone on down there the past couple of years. Boy, has Topsy got them all by the short hairs.

Well, nobody's coming in here one night and bashing me over the head.

"Rosebud."

Some joke, she thought ruefully, as she collapsed back onto the pillow.

❧

Veronica admired her nude reflection in the floor-to-ceiling mirror of her hotel bathroom. Veronica's back and Zoltan's got her. Reverse order, please. Zoltan's back and Veronica's got him. How charming he was on the phone half an hour ago. "Of course we have a deal, my dear." I'm sure none of those others trust me. Ruthelma's always hated my guts. Maybe now that she's married she's mellowed a bit. She's certainly made more on Seth than I ever did. More on him dead than when alive. *In Cold Water.* Poor old Seth. Are you in heaven? Have you found Ben Bentley? Are you perhaps together on Cloud Nine? I did love you, Seth. Please give me that. I really did love you. At times I even miss you.

You're getting sentimental, Veronica dear. That's a very bad sign. That means you're unsure of yourself and anxious. Mr. Auden insists this is the Age of Anxiety. It is also not the year of the Yearling. Veronica's a big girl now and a smart girl and she's playing with the grownups. She's as good as got her hands on half a million of Mr. Archimedes Zoltan's bucks. Once I get that publishing company going, I'll have the whole town groveling at my pedicured feet.

Why the sinking feeling in the pit of my stomach? What the hell was all that palaver last night at Ida's about murder? Why did Pharoah Love disappear?

"*Cat*."

Unconsciously, the fingers of both her hands formed claws.

Cat!

She made scratching gestures at her reflection and laughed.

So Topsy Alcott thinks she can outpoint everybody. That's a laugh. She hasn't seen little Veronica in action.

Murder.

She began shivering and quickly wrapped herself in a terry-cloth robe.

Murder.

I meant it when I said it. I've had enough of murder. But what if there's somebody else who hasn't had enough of murder?

I better watch my step.

◈

An hour after speaking on the telephone with Peter and Robert, Satan Stagg sat at his desk at the precinct house. Upon arrival, he had set in motion the tracer on "Rosebud." Then, to his surprise, he had been called into the office of his superior.

That was fifteen minutes ago.

His ears were still red from the impact of the tirade.

Lay off. Quit the case. It's closed. Leave it alone. Obey orders or else. This is from the top—not just me, but the *top*.

Like I suspected, they're closing in on me. And he suddenly blossomed with a rare, delightful, self-rewarding feeling of attainment. It's not that they're closing in on me.

It's that we're closing in on them.

He whistled merrily as he dialed his Aunt Hattie to wish her a Merry Christmas.

And don't forget little Satan, Santa. Many's the Christmas you did. But, please, not this one. Drop some more clues down my chimney. Place a few leads in my stretch sock.

Come on, Santa. Prove you're integrating.

9

"Do you suppose Raskalnikov might have really expired of velvet poisoning?"

Robert was minutely examining the décor of their new quarters in the Zoltan mansion. Peter was stretched on a chaise longue poring over the typewritten memorandum Robert had transcribed that morning from his notebook. Robert was darting back and forth across the room, examining the drapes, the wallpaper, the canopied bed, the pieces of furniture, like a representative from Sotheby's about to set a price.

"Oh, do light someplace," said Peter irritatedly. "You're giving me naupathia."

Robert shot him a quizzical look. "What's *that*?"

"Seasickness," said Peter with a smug look.

Robert ran his fingers along the wallpaper. "The

design is fascinating. Where's our magnifying glass?"

Peter spoke without looking up. "In my overnight case."

Robert crossed to the case, found the magnifying glass, returned to the wallpaper and examined it minutely. Though minus deerstalker cap and meerschaum pipe, he gave a fair representation of Sherlock Holmes.

"Peter," said Robert in a strange voice, "come look at this."

Peter sat up eagerly. "Bloodstain? Thumbprint?"

"Come look for yourself."

Peter crossed to him in two seconds, took the magnifying glass and examined the wallpaper. After several minutes of uh-huhing and "Well, well, well" in a variety of inflections, he straightened up and faced Robert. "*Mene, mene, tekel.* The handwriting on the wall. What a clever beggar, Raskalnikov. Those intricate little designs are a form of script!"

"But in what language?"

"Beats me." Both were lost in thought for several minutes. Then Peter broke the silence with a sharp snap of his fingers. "Igor. I'll bet the repulsive little creature with the hypertrophic neck can identify it."

"*Hypertrophic?*"

"Overdeveloped." Smugness dripped from Peter's voice again. "That'll teach you to scoff at Double-Crostics. Though one of these days if I ever lay my hands on Thomas H. Middleton, I shall throttle him. Now, how do we lure Igor into our parlor?"

"I'd much rather cross over to his."

"Meaning?"

"The old kill-a-couple-of-birds-with-one-stone bit. Don't you think it's a good idea to have Mother get Zoltan to arrange for us to be invited over to Topsy's this evening? After all, we're neighbors, and neighbors should be neighborly. One of us can find the opportunity to approach Igor, while the other attempts a meeting with the sequestered Jo."

"Robert, your ingenuity never ceases to amaze me. I'll ring for one of those Rudolph Friml footmen and get him to send Mother in here."

"Why don't you just cross the hall and knock at her door?"

"Really, Peter. That's not the way things are done in mansions."

❧

Mr. Rachel sipped his apéritif as he watched the Transylvanian ambassador rummaging through the papers on his desk. He thought to himself, Nicolu should have thought twice before dying his hair persimmon, but then Transylvania is such a small country they probably need to go to every extreme to excite some attention.

"I have found it," said Nicolu with a friendly smile as he extracted a small folder. "You realize, of course, this is extremely privileged information."

His voice took on a sly admonishment. "You promise never to reveal the source."

"You have my word," said Rachel, "and you know my word."

Nicolu nodded gravely. "Not a line about the orgies you have catered here has appeared in Suzy's column. You are a very honorable caterer." Rachel eyed the folder hungrily as Nicolu sat back and pressed his fingers together, a gesture Rachel recognized, one that would soon develop into a tiny game of pat-a-cake with himself in a style reminiscent of the late Hugh Herbert. "Strange. Very strange. A very quiet and underhanded attempt was made to have this Isogul deported from this country a little over a year ago."

"Really? Not by Guru Raskalnikov, by any chance?"

"Oh, no. It was Raskalnikov who thwarted the action. The mechanism was set in motion by the formidable Topsy Alcott."

I'm tingling. Rachel had months ago caught Ruthelma's infection.

"Regardless, Transylvania wanted no part of this traitor." Nicolu divorced the fingertips and tapped the folder. "It was Raskalnikov who secured Isogul's visa and brought him to America."

"How fascinating!"

"Yes." He lifted the folder and held it out to Rachel. "What you have here is a Xerox copy. I trust you will see to it that this document does not fall into the wrong hands. If it does and there are repercussions, you understand I will have to accuse you of having formally stolen this during a friendly visit."

Rachel took the document and placed it in his briefcase. "My deepest gratitude, Nicolu."

"I do not like Topsy Alcott. When I go to her Tara Club, she gives me a rotten table. Even Monaco does better. But then, our princes have no opportunity of marrying movie stars. Those lousy vampire movies frighten them away from Transylvania. I shall call on you soon to cater another orgy. Keep May thirtieth open. It is your Memorial Day. We too appreciate something memorable on Memorial Day." Nicolu winked, and Rachel downed the apéritif.

⋘⊰⊱⋙

In five hours, Satan had accumulated an impressive file of Rosebuds. He studied each Rosebud Company that had come in over the wire, but none struck him as bearing any connection to Archimedes Zoltan. There were Rosebud Cement and Gravel, Rosebud Wigs and Perukes, Rosebud Orthopedics, Rosebud Rosebuds, even Rosebud Incense and Thermibles. The list looked as though it belonged on the bottom of one of the back pages of *The New Yorker*. "Bring it all with you," Robert had said to him on the phone. Goodness, Aunt Hattie, your nephew is going up in the world. He's been invited to tea at a mansion. He hopes he remembers to use the front door.

⋘⊰⊱⋙

"Now, Jo," cajoled Ada Bergheim, "hold still and let me tie this bow in your hair. A pretty pink velvet bow for your pretty yellow hair."

Pink on yellow, Jo thought to herself with distaste. I'll look like the wrapping on a box of Barton's chocolates. Who's Topsy bringing up here, anyway? She's been firm about no visitors, but today she suddenly decides to put me on display. I know Zoltan's back, but Zoltan's different. He's not *company*. He's the whole shmear.

Why hasn't Beth been in to see me? It's way past luncheon. She always comes in and reads to me. She thinks I don't understand any of it. She does it only because she thinks that's the sort of service you should give an invalid even if the invalid's a dummy. Well, I'm not a dummy. I see, I hear, and I understand. I even felt some life in my fingers today. That shattered nerve in my skull is beginning to heal. I know it. It's got to. But they mustn't know it. I played that stupid blinking game with Nursie for an hour this morning. She's asking for trouble. She continues to direct all her questions toward Topsy. She seems to have given up on Igor for the time being. She thinks Igor frightens me. It wasn't mentioning Pharoah that frightened me. It was what he tried to remove from the closet. That was pretty dumb of him. Unless . . .

"What is it, dear?" asked Ada anxiously as Jo's brow furrowed, "is there something you're trying to tell me?"

Jo blinked her eyes No and settled her face into its usual bland expression.

Almost gave myself away then. Igor's afraid. That's it. He's afraid. Would they dare? Would they dare do anything to him? But they wouldn't. Another murder could blow the whole caper sky high. Dear God, hurry. Heal that nerve. I've got to get out of here. My days are numbered. I can feel it. I sense it. I can see it in Topsy's face. Something's going wrong. Is it that broad Zoltan's going to marry? Is that who they're bringing up to see me? Step right up, ladies and gentlemen, and see the freak!

"Tears!" exclaimed Ada. "What's wrong? Why are you crying? Does it hurt someplace?"

"*Urgle gurgle urgle gurgle . . .*"

❧

The young footman gently shut the door behind him as he left the Raskalnikov room. What a household, he thought to himself. That gruesome Zoltan, that dizzy Cartier broad, and now these twins. Mineral water in one room. Champagne in another. Daiquiris, apéritifs and seven and seven in this room. An old queen with pompadoured hair. A spook who smokes cigarillos. Why'd I ever break my ankle and have to quit the Ice Capades?

❧

Peter, Robert, Mr. Rachel and Satan sat in a circle around the table on which rested their drinks, the Rosebud list and the Igor Isogul folder.

"We're progressing," said Robert assuredly. "We're definitely progressing."

"I couldn't see a lead in those Rosebuds," admitted Satan after a quick swig of his seven and seven.

"Nor I," agreed Peter.

"No negative thinking today," admonished Robert. "Let's get to the stuff on Igor." He opened the folder and began reading to himself, the others watching his face for any telltale reactions. They were rewarded immediately.

"Listen to this," said Robert eagerly. " 'Igor Isogul, born May 26, 1903. Parents: father was Bela Isogul, a notorious anarchist, and mother's maiden name was Selma . . .' " He paused and then said with shattering emphasis, " '*Zoltan*.' "

"Hello hello hello-o-o-o," whispered Peter. Satan edged forward in his seat. Mr. Rachel's fingers tightened around his snifter.

Robert continued. " 'Igor Isogul was an only child. He attended the University of Transylvania, where he majored in biochemistry, romance languages and political science. At the university he met and married a fellow student, Wera Shrdlu, a major in journalism. The marriage took place on July 28, 1923, and three weeks later they were blessed with the birth of a son? Oh, my God, it's too much!"

Robert leaped to his feet with skyrockets exploding in his eyes.

"For God's sake, Robert!" cried Peter. "What is it?"

"The son's name. Here, see for yourselves—*Guru* Isogul!"

In turn, each grabbed the folder and read the name for himself. Satan looked at the ceiling and whispered gratefully, "Thank you, Santa." With an effort at self-control, Robert took his seat again, the folder was returned to him and he resumed reading.

" 'Igor and Wera became staunch Communists, etcetera etcetera etcetera, and on various occasions served jail sentences on suspicion of subversive activities.' " He looked up. "It must have taken a bit of doing, getting Igor into this country with that background."

"Keep reading," said Peter impatiently.

" 'During one prolonged incarceration, the well-being of their son was entrusted to Selma Isogul's brother. The brother, a gamekeeper on the estates of an uncle in the Carpathian mountains, was accidentally shot and killed during a hunt when mistaken for a wapiti by *his* uncle, who then assumed the care of the boy.' Oh, God. Here it is and I feel faint. The name of this uncle, the boy's great-uncle—Archimedes Zoltan!"

"The mind goggles," whispered Rachel and downed the apéritif.

"He must be in his nineties," commented an awestruck Satan.

"Poor Mumsy," said Peter.

"Then it goes on to detail how Igor and Wera attempted to assassinate Herman Goering during a state visit, and full marks for them on that score, were captured, brought to trial, and condemned to death by hanging. Wera swallowed a poison capsule and succumbed, and Igor faced the punishment alone. Of course we know he survived, made his living as a tinker going from village to village like something out of Bernard Malamud, then managed to contact his son, now an adult and living"—Robert smiled—"in great luxury in the United States." He let the folder slip from his fingers and it landed on the table. "And the rest we know. Now, gentlemen, I find it awfully hard to believe that Igor murdered his own son. Also, if he knew the identity of the murderer, he would have spilled the beans long ago."

"Not necessarily," said Satan, and he stubbed out his cigarillo in an ashtray and began groping in his pocket for his pipe. "We know that Topsy tried to have Igor deported *prior* to Raskalnikov's murder, which means Igor was already some kind of fly in her ointment. But Raskalnikov managed to nip that piece of treachery in the bud. Possibly with Zoltan's help, he being Igor's uncle. Whatever Igor knows, I figure the price for his silence was continued sanctuary here in the States. But I'll tell you what I think Igor *does* know. Two things. One, the murder weapon. And two, some of the secrets of international financial transactions Guru never got around to spilling to the old man. And I'll lay odds the answers to that one are on the wallpaper." He sat back, lit a match, applied it to his pipe, and basked in the glow of their admiration at his swift deductions.

"Satan," said Robert, "you make admirable sense. We've got to get to Igor and make him trust us and translate that wallpaper."

"And the weapon," added Peter, "don't forget the weapon." He tapped the list Satan had brought with him. "Rosebud."

Robert leaned forward. "Peter? Are you insinuating Rosebud has something to do with the weapon?"

"Uh huh. Let's go back over that list and see if any of those companies manufactures anything that would make a formidable weapon. By the process of intelligent elimination, we ought to come up with a few likely possibilities."

Mr. Rachel cleared his throat. "Might a mere mortal ask a seemingly innocent question? If the wallpaper hieroglyphics, or whatever in the name of heaven those things are, contain secrets that have been, as you think, Satan, held back from Zoltan, why were they necessarily held back? In other words, was Guru double-crossing Zoltan, or was it merely his extremely clever method of listing all *previous* transactions where no one would think of looking for them in the event of Zoltan's sudden death? In *other* words, does Zoltan possibly know the meaning of the handwriting on the wall, and no pun intended, and was this method conceived because of a possible mutual distrust shared by Zoltan and Raskalnikov for possibly someone named, shall we say, Topsy Alcott, and, good God, how I'm tingling."

Satan leaned over and kissed Rachel's cheek.

"Thank you," Rachel said shyly, and then thought to himself, But I hope you know I never cheat on my beloved Ruthelma.

Robert spoke. "Then Igor's brazen behavior can be attributed to Topsy's desperate need for information she suspects Igor and only Igor can supply her with. Do you suppose we're right?"

"We'd better be," said Satan. "It's all we've got."

Peter's face was a study. "Conspirators, take heed. I still think Igor's days on his catbird perch might be numbered. If, as Satan thinks, Topsy's getting worried that we're closing in on her, she'd sooner save her neck then add to her savings. The secret information becomes expendable, and Igor, who's been living on borrowed time anyway, gets the source of his loan abruptly amputated and it's goodbye Igor. And if it's goodbye Igor, it's goodbye us. He's our only definite lead to the identity of Rosebud. Now, Mother has maneuvered us an invitation to cocktails in the home of the queen bee and her drones in approximately an hour. We've got to maneuver Igor aside at some point and somehow gain his confidence."

"There's safety in numbers," contributed Robert, "and the more the merrier. The invitation didn't positively say we couldn't bring a friend. I'm bringing Satan. Peter, Mr. Rachel's your date. Between us, at the end of the cocktail hour, we should hang our heads in shame if we're unable to consider our mission accomplished. Now let's start narrowing down that list of Rosebuds."

❧

Zoltan was comfortably settled in his portable throne chair, and Madeleine sat at his feet with her legs folded under her reading from *In Cold Water*.

"Magnificent writing," fifed Zoltan. "So precise,

so clean-cut, such economy of words and yet what a wealth of underlying emotion. Such sad people, this Seth Piro and Pharoah Love. You knew them both."

"I adored them," said Madeleine sadly. "I think of Seth often, even if he was instrumental in nailing Mama as Sweet Harriet's murderer. Pharoah was another kettle of fish. A bit of an enigma. I wonder where he's disappeared to. He was quite chummy with Topsy and some of her household, you know."

"I know. And Guru. When are we due at Topsy's for cocktails?"

"In about an hour. Shall I read a bit more?"

Zoltan gestured her to continue. She read for another ten minutes and stopped when a series of cluck-cluck-clucks were emitted from Zoltan's mouth. Madeleine looked up.

"How beautifully they build their suspense. Your twins are extremely talented, Madeleine." She puffed up with pride. "Of course, they lack some of the power of my favorite author, Sheridan Le Fanu."

"Sheridan who? The only Sheridans I'm familiar with are General and Ann. Arkie . . ."

"What."

"Are my boys on the spot?"

"What spot?"

"Are they in danger?" She shut the book and put it aside. "We're not fools, my boys and I. And I'm not as scatterbrained as I sometimes mislead people to suspect. Last night Topsy openly threatened them. Not unsubtly, of course, but a threat's a threat. I've been on the receiving end of a great many and I know one when I hear one. You must promise me, Arkie, nothing will happen to my boys."

"Topsy moves in mysterious ways, mysterious even to me who have been associated with her for several decades."

"Are you trying to tell me there are certain areas in which you can't control her?"

"Topsy is a very particular and very peculiar woman. We were lovers once."

"That's not news."

"She is also a very ambitious woman. Her appetite can never be sated."

"In other words, nothing stands in her way, including you."

"I recently reached that disturbing conclusion."

"Then why don't you get rid of her?"

His alabaster eyes penetrated her like laser beams. "I still need her."

"What happens to your empire after you're gone?"

He said nothing.

"Is Topsy in line to take over?"

His silence continued.

"Well, if she's not in line, do you suppose she's been planning to put herself in line?"

No answer.

"Why don't you knock twice if it's Yes?"

"Stay out of my affairs, Madeleine. To attempt to understand the complex intricacies of my financial network is an impossibility. Other than myself, only Guru could. And that died with him. When I die, it dies with me. Unless there is time to train another Guru, and that takes years. Guru was with me from the time he was ten years of age. It took two decades to instruct him. I do not have two decades in which to instruct another."

"How about my boys?" suggested Madeleine brightly. "They're pretty quick on the uptake, and they adore money."

"Madeleine," said Zoltan wearily, "read."

Madeleine resumed reading, but though her eyes translated the written word to the spoken word, her mind was busy elsewhere. My betrothed, she soon decided, is nuts.

"Nuts?" piccoloed Zoltan.

"Did I say nuts?"

"I distinctly heard you say 'Nuts,' and it seems completely out of context with what you've been reading."

"Perhaps I did say 'Nuts.' I'm a bit hungry. I think I'll ring for some nuts."

"Have them sent to your room, Madeleine. I would like to rest a bit before joining you for cocktails at Topsy's."

"Shall I leave the book?"

"Please."

She placed it in his lap, kissed his alabaster forehead and left the room.

Topsy openly threatened them . . . areas in which you can't control her . . . nothing stands in her way, including you.

Including me.

Ruthelma slammed the phone down angrily. Has the *magic* gone out of our *lives?*

She marched to the kitchen in cadence to her angry muttering, opened the refrigerator, pulled out the square box that contained a Reuben's strawberry cheesecake, crossed to the table, appropriating a kitchen knife from the washbasin en route, and, still muttering, sat and attacked the cheesecake the way Theseus went for the Minotaur.

I'm *talking* to myself *again.* I *must* stop talking to *myself.* Why *should* I? It's the *only* time I receive *intelligent* answers.

They're going to *Topsy's* for cocktails and *I* stay at home eating *cheesecake.* Aren't *I* a part of this entente *cordiale?* What's so *cordiale* about this *entente* if I'm left at *home* like this and on *Christmas* Day?

The first slice of cheesecake disappeared down her throat faster than a shovelful of bituminous down a coal chute.

And they have *leads.* But, oh *no,* can *Rachel* tell *me?* Oh *no.* Someone might be *listening* on an *extension.* I have to *wait* till he comes *home.*

Well, *we'll* see about *that.*

ঙঞ্চৈ

The break in Guru's neck throbbed with a dull pain. It always did when he sensed danger to himself, and today the pain was at its most intense.

He patted his inside jacket pocket and felt a momentary warmth from the security of the envelopes securely placed in it. His bonus from Topsy. His bonuses from Amy and Meg. There was still a collection due from Beth.

She didn't appear at breakfast. She didn't appear at lunch. She hasn't even sent for a tray. Why has she kept to her room all day? She didn't appear at the Christmas tree to receive her gifts and join Topsy, Meg and Beth, with the servants singing Christmas carols. Such Christmas carols. "We're in the Money." "With Plenty of Money and You." And "Something's Got to Give."

And Madame's guest remains secluded in her room. Very strange.

He pressed the palm of his hand against his neck, but the pain persisted.

I am in danger. Do they dare?

⋘⧽⧽

Beth sat at a window of her darkened room, staring out at the black sky. I used to hate the winter because it got dark so early. Now I love it. I need the darkness tonight. I need the cover for my getaway. And I need Igor. Where the hell's that blackmailing son of a bitch? Doesn't he want his bonus? I've got a little extra for him, too. If he'll steal the keys to the Volks from Meg's room I'll give him my engagement ring. I can't let go of my cash. It'll be months before I dare hock anything. Topsy'll know how to trace that. She has a list of all our jewelry. She has a list of everything we own.

Thank God she told me to stay in my room. Sure I look awful, Topsy. You ought to know. It's thanks to you.

Come on, Igor. I need a head start upstate. It'll be hours before they miss me. Come on, Igor. Just this once, I'm aching for the sight of you.

There was a brusque rap at her door.

Beth arose, crossed to the door and asked, "Who is it?"

"Itttt issss Igorrrrrr. Season'sssss greetingsssss."

10

HIS EYES opened slowly, and with an effort he brought them into focus. He was lying face down across the bed, his head hanging over the edge. On the floor *In Cold Water* lay where it must have dropped when he collapsed.

Collapse? But that is impossible. Not yet. Not this soon. I was guaranteed time. Goldberg assured me there would still be time. Then what is going wrong? Why did I black out? How long have I been lying here? Cocktails. Cocktails at Topsy's. Madeleine would have found me if I'd been lying here longer than an hour.

He looked at the grandfather's clock (assuredly, he'd been guaranteed, Alexander Hamilton's grandfather) at the opposite side of the room. He'd been blacked out less than ten minutes.

Zoltan rolled over on his back. He was drenched

with perspiration. He could hear the sounds of escaping steam, and then realized it was himself wheezing. He was wheezing in B-flat minor and he knew that signaled danger.

Goldberg. Goldberg. You deceived me. Maugham and Churchill, you said, could have added another ten years to their lives if they had followed the strict regimen advised by their doctors of your rival sanitarium. No brandy. No cigars. No martinis. A bland diet. *I* listened. *I* obeyed.

He struggled in his pants pocket, found the handkerchief and mopped at his brow.

Treachery. Everywhere treachery.

You were bought, Goldberg. You were bought. You diluted my injections. You shot into my near-atrophied veins only a sufficient amount to carry me across the ocean, into this mansion, into Topsy's hands.

Had he been studying himself in a looking glass, he would have recognized the smirk on his face. It was the one of begrudging admiration.

I taught you well, Topsy. I took a clever hatcheck girl out of a cloakroom and created an evil empress. I bear you no grudge, Topsy. But I bear you no gifts, either.

Oh, God! Is this the end of Zoltan?

Tant pis.

Will they be there to greet me, those whose dispatch I've hastened? Enesco, my nephew, whom I said I mistook for a wapiti. Wera, who innocently swallowed what she thought was a capsule of vitamin B1. *"To give you strength, dear. The strength to face the gallows."* Goering swallowed that one, too. And so many others. So many, many others.

He stroked his chin with trembling fingers.

Blackout. This is the first. There will be three. And then the end of an era. I swore if I can't take it with me I won't go. But I *shall* take it with me. My wonderfully funny friend with the red bulbous nose taught me well over those many games of pool we shot together. *"Keep it out of the hands of those vultures. Eight ball in the side pocket."*

Billions in unnumbered accounts. Billions in banks across the world under pseudonyms. Genghis X. Fleedlegoggle. Joachim T. Fleapowder. Marcus T. Neimann. What fun I've had! And you'll never find them, Topsy. You'll never know.

And walls can't talk.

I'll see to that. I'll see to that at once.

❧

"Hello hello hello-o-o-o-o-o!" Madeleine entered wearing a monkey-skin dress cut eight inches above the knee, a vertigo-inducing plunged neckline, a ruby choker around her neck and two illegal egret feathers protruding from her curls. "Oh, Arkie!" The dismay in her voice might have been Jacqueline Kennedy's on chance-encountering William Manchester. "You're not even ready!"

Zoltan found the strength with which to sit up and prop himself against the headboard. He had first retrieved *In Cold Water*, and now he placed it on his lap.

"Madeleine," he tweetled, "inasmuch as I do not drink, I find cocktail parties tiresome. Will you excuse me and extend my regrets to Topsy?"

"*Arkie.*"

His piccolo voice rose a treble. "Madeleine. Do as I tell you." He forced a twinkle into each eye. "When you return, we shall have a cozy tête à tête alone in your rooms. A quiet dinner of cold pheasant in aspic and, for you, bottles of bubbly bubbly bubbly."

Madeleine crossed her hands across her chest, closed her eyes and conjured up a dreamy expression for her face. "Oh, Arkie. How romantic!" (A similar moment almost won me the Academy Award when I played Camille. Of course, in my version there was none of that crappy coughing herself to death. My Camille wound up playing piano in a sleazy waterfront cafe in Marseilles singing "It Had to Be You" and drinking absinthe. I'll never understand why Bosley Crowther hated it.)

"Madeleine?"

"Hmmmmm?"

"Are you falling asleep on your feet?"

"Oh no no no no no," she cadenzaed gaily, "I was just momentarily paralyzed with delight." She crossed to the bed, sat down, put her arms around Zoltan and kissed his alabaster cheek. "Why, Arkie! Your cheek's so clammy and you're soaking wet! Have you caught a chill?" She chucked him under the chin and he winced as one of her nails scraped his skin. "You're not feeling well, are you?"

"Madeleine." He spoke her name with the weariness of Hanley Stafford admonishing Baby Snooks. "You will notice the room is overheated, and therefore I am overheated. When you are gone, I shall indulge in a lukewarm tub, scent myself with attar of ficoid, sip a glass of hot water and lemon, and then eagerly await your return from Topsy's. Now, don't keep them waiting, Peter and . . . and . . ."

Something's wrong, thought Madeleine, something's very very wrong. He's wet. His skin is clammy. His hands are trembling. And he can't remember Robert's name.

". . . and . . . Robert. Yes . . . Robert." He didn't realize how hard was the grip on the book in his lap.

Madeleine had risen and was standing staring into his face. Her voice was gentle when she spoke. "I won't be long, Arkie. I'll just have one drink and come right back to you. Shall I send a footman to draw your bath?"

He shook his head slowly from side to side. "I want to be alone."

Later, when she was alone with the twins, Satan and Mr. Rachel on their way to Topsy's duplex, dramatically re-creating the brief but disturbing interlude with Zoltan, she would recall with amazement that she had tiptoed from the room and, for some inexplicable reason, had to fight to hold back her tears.

Alone, Zoltan thought to himself, She is a sweet woman. Star-crossed but sweet. I must provide for her. One decent gesture before I go. With an effort, he moved toward the telephone on his night table and dialed his attorney.

"Louis?" he tweetled into the phone. "This is

Zoltan. Forgive me for disturbing you today of all days, but I wish to add a new codicil to my will. Will you write it down, please, type it up and send it around to me in the morning for my signature. Thank you Louis."

Igor crouched unseen, with one hand pressed against his aching neck, in a dark recess of the corridor on the third floor of the duplex. He saw Topsy enter Jo's room, heard a brief and unimportant conversation with the nurse, saw the nurse emerge into the corridor, a perplexed expression on her face as she crossed to the staircase and descended. Then at the end of the corridor he saw the door to the guest suite open.

A pussycat? For a moment he forgot the pain in his neck as he watched Ocelot glide stealthily to Jo's room.

So that is Ocelot. Why does she hide behind the mask? Why does she wear that strange leopard-skin leotard and ballet slippers? Would I know the face behind that mask? I shall listen at the keyhole. Perhaps I shall add another weapon to the arsenal in my brain.

Ocelot entered Jo's room and shut the door. Igor looked around cautiously, then scurried to the door and knelt with his ear to the keyhole.

Topsy stood smiling behind the chair in which Jo sat limply, as Ocelot entered, closed the door, and leaned against it for a moment.

Control, thought Jo to herself, control. They

can't hear my heart pressing against my ribs. I know who this is. I know why she's been brought to this house. There's still hope. The nerve is healing. There's life in my fingers again. There was movement in my leg. And my brain is more alert than ever. Stay limp. Don't tense. Relax. Relax. Those talons on her gloves. Ten razors. They wouldn't dare do anything now. There's company expected for cocktails. Ada told me. Zoltan and Madeleine Cartier and her sons. She's only come to look me over and gauge. To see if I'm still a vegetable. Show her you're still a vegetable.

"*Urgle gurgle urgle gurgle.*"

Topsy chirruped to Ocelot, "That means she's glad to see you!"

Slowly Ocelot advanced across the room, removing the taloned glove from her right hand. Soon she stood looking down at Jo.

"Hello, kitten." Gently she stroked Jo's cheek. "You're more beautiful than ever. I wanted to see you. It's been so many months since I saw you." She knelt at Jo's side and took a limp hand and pressed it to her lips.

Jo flinched slightly. Damn, she thought to herself. Control, you idiot, control. So what if those frigging whiskers tickle?

Ocelot laughed. "My whiskers tickled her."

Topsy cocked her head slightly. "Really."

Ocelot reached up to Jo's chin and moved her head for a better look at her. "I can't believe it, kitten. The doctors say there's no hope. But I can't believe it. You had more strength than any of us. But it's better this way. For all of us. Even for you." She straightened up. "All right, Topsy kitten. I've seen enough. She's unharmed and still beautiful. And I want to cry. Let's go."

Igor scurried away from the door, back to the cover of the stygian recess. And in time. The door to Jo's room opened and Ocelot emerged, and at the same moment Ada reached the head of the landing carrying a tray with a cup of custard and a glass of milk. Ada came face to face with Ocelot, who reared back with a meow of surprise. Ada gasped and the tray crashed to the floor. Topsy came running from Jo's room, saw the tray and its contents on the floor, saw Ocelot rush to the guest room and disappear into it, saw the astonished and slightly clever look on Ada's face, and knew there was no stopping the raging torrent of blood coloring her face.

"You stupid bitch!" shouted Topsy. "I said ten minutes!"

Ada's head angled bravely. "It *was* ten minutes, and that's no way to speak to a registered nurse. I'll ring for Igor to clear up this mess."

Igor had carefully edged his way to the head of the back stairs, and now emerged from the shadows.

"Igorrrr issss here."

Topsy spun on her heel.

"What are you doing here? You've been spying again!"

"Igorrrr justttt come upppppp backkkk staircase. Igorrrrr seekkkkkk Mah-dommmmm. Guestsssss willlll soonnnnn arrive."

Topsy turned to Ada. "Go to Jo. Igor will bring

171

up a new tray." Ada moved past her into Jo's room and shut the door.

So what if they've seen Ocelot, thought Topsy hastily. She'll be on public display in a few nights, anyway. Why am I so on edge since she got here? Beating up on Beth the way I did. Cursing the nurse the way I did. I've got to regain my cool. The enemy will soon be entering the fortress and there's no repelling them with flaming arrows and vats of boiling oil. I've got to move carefully. Very carefully. My best mistress-of-the-house smile. My lovely-hostess façade. The way I greet the suckers who come to Tara.

When she spoke, she was delighted to hear the words ripple forth like a sylvan stream. "Clean up this mess, Igor, then bring a fresh tray to Jo's room. And knock without entering. Nurse will come to the door for the tray."

Igor's angled head bobbed up and down like a Yo-Yo.

"Later, see if Beth needs anything. She's not been feeling well."

Igor smiled.

Smile, you venomous little bastard, smile. Topsy's got the eraser with which to wipe it from your face forever.

Regally she turned and descended the stairs.

≈§≈

A fit of trembling seized Ada the moment she was safe in Jo's room. That cat thing's eyes. They met mine briefly, but the memory of them is as indelible as a sailor's tattoo. I've seen eyes like that

172

before. I know I have. But where? Whom did they belong to? So what if I finally ràn into that Ocelot—what's to get into such a shit snit about? Topsy's nervous. Topsy's tense. And she's been letting down that iron guard of hers. What went on in this room in my absence? She crossed to Jo.

"Jo. Do you hear me?"

Oh, Christ. Here we go again. Blinkety blink blink. *Really.* The way Topsy said it after Ocelot said the whiskers tickled me. She suspects. She suspects there's feeling in my hand again. If I could only say the same for my tongue. To articulate again. But I can articulate. My eyelids. If I could only be sure of my Florence Nightingale. Maybe she's genuine. Maybe she's for real. I heard Topsy call her a stupid bitch. I heard Ada's bristling reply. Maybe she's not one of Topsy's spies after all. Maybe I can trust her. Goddammit, I *have* to trust her.

Ada was kneeling at her side. "Jo," she persisted. "Don't you hear me?"

Jo blinked and then slowly raised her right hand.

"My God," whispered Ada. "My God. It's like Lourdes! It's a miracle!"

Jo's hand beckoned to Ada as tears filled her eyes and a look of beseechment spread across her vegetable face.

Ada took Jo's hand and clung to it. "I understand, darling. I understand. Now, calmly . . . calmly . . . let's get to work."

⌘

Ocelot stood at the French windows, staring down into the garden and abstractedly stroking her leotard. Really, kitten, that was a dumb thing to do, she admonished herself. You should have nodded politely to the white sister instead of going into shock like Adam Clayton Powell faced with a process server. Well, dearie, she did take you by surprise, and vice versa. I'm not as self-assured as I ought to be. It was different in those tank towns these past six months. We were all strangers to each other there and I had the confidence of my anonymity. But this is New York. This is the big time, baby. You'll be a celebrity. There'll be interviews and television appearances and you have to conduct yourself like something special, which you are. You can't turn tail and run any longer. You have to face up to everyone and everything. That's part of the new life.

You mustn't let anyone guess that sometimes your insides crumble like stale Nabiscos. That sometimes your knees quake like Manton Moreland's in those crummy Monogram pictures. That you think too often the jig's up, like they said at so many lynchings. You must walk with pride and dignity and inner belief, because now you're a lady.

Nobody asked you to join the grownups at cocktails. So what? *You* are *Ocelot. You* go where you *choose* to go. Get into that panther outfit and stalk your way downstairs like the brazen hussy you really are at heart.

Remember what the psychiatrist told you.

"You must act differently, think differently,

feel differently. Then and only then will the transition you desire succeed. Do you feel yourself capable of this?"

You bet your ass, Buster.

◆⧉◆

Small talk, chitchat, mots and an occasional witticism fell on Topsy's living room like pamphlets dropping over Hanoi calling for surrender. Meg and Amy passed among the guests with canapés and hors d'oeuvres, Meg seeing to it that Peter got more than his share of the smoked salmon. No sign of Beth, mused Peter. No sign of Topsy, mused Robert. What was that commotion on the upper floor as we arrived? mused Satan. It's a bore and Ruthelma's not missing a thing, mused Mr. Rachel. Could the boys be right? mused a worried Madeleine. Is it senility? Is it the first signs I saw in him, lying so clammy and drenched on the bed? The way D. W. Griffith appeared on that last visit before he expired. If they're right in their supposition that this means Topsy will be forced to move quickly, too quickly to think carefully, so quickly that the serious error will be made that just might lead to Raskalnikov's murderer—if they're right, does this mean bloodshed? Where the hell is she, anyway? And what an entrance that'll be.

"Hello hellooo hello-o-o-o-o-o-o-o!"

Madeleine cringed. The imitation was acid perfection itself. Topsy entered the room with arms outstretched. *"Joyeux Noël!* But where's Zoltan?"

"He sends his regrets," caroled Madeleine as she moved lithely toward the outstreched arms, deciding to forgo any further explanation for Zoltan's absence. "My dear, you look absolutely ravished." Topsy's skin turned ashen. "Or do I mean 'ravishing'?" Madeleine zeroed in between Topsy's outstretched arms and planted a peck on her left cheek with an overstressed "Mmmmmmwahhhhh."

Topsy moved back, held Madeleine at arm's length and surveyed the monkey-furred outfit. "What simian symmetry!"

"I'm glad you like it," said Madeleine with an ice-cubes-against-glass tinkle. "I got it in North Africa. It was designed by Lady Greystoke."

Topsy turned to the men. "Gentlemen! And what a surprise, Mr. Stagg and Mr. Rachel. I adore surprises." She crossed to each and bestowed a kiss on their cheeks like a butterfly side-swiping cornstalks. "Oh, do sit down, all of you."

"And where's your daughter Beth?" Satan's smile more than made up for the dim luster in the eyes of Topsy, Meg and Amy. "We had a delightful chat at Ida's very, very early this morning."

"Meg," said Topsy, "my Sazerac." She crossed and sat opposite Satan. "Beth's not at all well. I suppose it's no use shielding the fact any longer. There have been hints in Suzy Knickerbocker's and Doris Lilley's columns. Beth drinks a bit too much."

"Like her daddy?" queried Satan. "She talked an awful lot about her daddy."

"Let's forget Beth. This is Christmas. It's a festive day. Let's speak of festive things." Topsy turned to Madeleine. "Have you and Zoltan chosen a wedding day?"

Madeleine crossed her legs and knit her fingers around her knee. "When we do, you'll be the first to know."

"And Mr. Rachel." He was caught with a mouthful of canape. "Are wheels spinning for New Year's Eve?"

Rachel swallowed, gasped for air and then replied, "Wheels are most certainly spinning."

Robert decided on a plunge. "I wonder if I could have a few moments with your butler Igor."

"Why?" It slashed at his ear.

"We've had a magnificent stroke of luck today. Some information more or less fell into our hands. It seems there was a deeper relation between Igor and Raskalnikov than merely butler and employer."

Amy held tightly to Meg's hand. Topsy played with the string of pearls around her neck, and for a moment Madeleine would have sworn it seemed about to tighten like a noose.

"They were father and son," Topsy said and applauded herself at the ease with which the sentence emerged. It did not deflate Robert.

"You know, then, that Zoltan is Guru's great-uncle."

Topsy shifted in her seat. "Does Zoltan know you're aware of all this?"

"Does it matter?"

Topsy's lips formed a moue, and then she spoke. "Zoltan abhors all invasions of privacy. Where did you get this information?"

"I'm not at liberty to say."

"But you're at liberty to pry and destroy and

cruelly expose private lives for the sake of a catch-penny enterprise."

"More importantly," interjected Satan, "there's a murderer to be apprehended. Don't interrupt me. You and your associates have obstructed justice for exactly one year. And don't remind me that I'm sticking my tongue out at the law laid down to me by the great white father back at the precinct. I got other strings to my bow if they bounce me off the force for insubordination. We're here for one reason and for one reason only. We're going to collar Raskalnikov's killer, and the boys are going to write their book. Lady, take a leaf from my Aunt Hattie's book of homilies: If you can't beat 'em, join 'em."

"I select my own allies," rejoindered Topsy, her temperature at boiling point. "And you can tell the Transylvanian ambassador he shall most certainly be recalled!"

"Why'd you try to have Igor deported?" asked Peter swiftly.

"I never—" She caught herself. "No point in denying that now, is there?" Her eyes darted to the entrance to the pantry as Igor emerged bearing a tray of hot canapés. "I didn't ring for you!"

"These willll currrrdddddllle."

"Hello, Igor" said Peter amiably. "We were just talking about you. And your Uncle Zoltan and your son Guru."

The tray clattered to the floor and Rachel looked with distaste at his canapé-spattered shoes. Igor clutched at his neck and his eyes signaled hatred toward Topsy, who jumped to her feet shouting, "Get out! Get out! All of you! Get out! Amy! Meg! Get them out of here!"

And then a black panther stalked into the room, her panther's tail draped loosely over her left wrist, a cigarette and holder poised between the fingers of her right hand, and a feline expression on her face. "Am I interrupting?"

Topsy went white. Amy fumbled in the pocket of her dress for her pin. Meg murmured under her breath, "Gahhhd." Madeleine's jaw dropped. For some inexplicable reason Peter thought to himself, *Déjà vu*. Robert felt the hairs at the back of his neck stiffen. Igor bent slowly and picked up the tray. And like a true gentleman of the old school, Mr. Rachel got to his feet and bowed from the waist.

"My name's Ocelot," she purred. "What's yours?"

11

THE VARIETY of tableaux at the Women's Rehabilitation Institute during the cocktail hour would have brought joy and inspiration to Hieronymus Bosch and Hogarth. Mad Myrtle MacGruder held court in her private suite, having first called for her pipe, her slippers and her fiddlers three. The majority of her wards were still feeling the aftereffects of the special Christmas dinner served three hours earlier. The menu had been carefully culled from *The Alice B. Toklas Cookbook*, and though the roast loin of elephant had been done to perfection, its richness almost succeeded in finishing off half of the Institute's population.

Bromo-Seltzers, Alka-Seltzers and antacid pills were being slipped from cell to cell with the alacrity usually reserved for pot, junk and Bandaids. The hardier and sturdier held wrestling matches, boxing exhibitions and shot-put demonstrations, with the smallest of the ladies as the reluctant shots.

Only one cell boasted an air of decorum.

Fauna sat at the edge of her cot staring into the tiny crystal ball she clutched in her right hand, a birthday gift from Peter and Robert, who had relished the consternation its selection had caused at Hammacher-Schlemmer's. She moved her left hand in a slow rotation over the ball, whispering first a chant, then several imprecations, and finally two choruses of "I See Your Face Before Me."

"*Madeleine*," Fauna whispered. "I see Madeleine . . . and the *twins*."

The box of Goobers dropped from Flora's hand, and the chocolate-covered nuts scattered across the floor. Winnie Ruth nervously pulled at her bottle of sake, one of Mad Myrtle's more thoughtful Christmas offerings.

Fauna's face contorted in agony. "The ball's so hot . . . so hot . . . it's burning my hand."

"Drop it, baby," cautioned Flora.

Fauna stifled a cry of pain.

"Horribre!"

"Flames!" shrieked Fauna.

"Frames!" echoed Winnie Ruth with an entreating look at Flora.

"They're in danger of flames!" Fauna now bounced the crystal ball back and forth. "I see conflagration and tragedy and destruction!"

"Oh, Rord."

Flora could restrain herself no longer. She lunged forward and caught the crystal ball and held it behind her back. It was ice cold to the touch.

Fauna clenched her hands together and looked up at Flora beseechingly. "They don't know the danger! They've got to be warned!"

"Terephone!"

"The mansion's unlisted," stormed Flora, now pacing the cell, "if they're there at all. How desperate is the danger, baby? Can it wait till tomorrow when we make our break?"

"Tomorrow will be too late," whined Fauna. "Too late."

"Too rate."

Flora tossed the crystal ball onto her bunk, folded her arms akimbo and stared down at Winnie Ruth. "We've got to get out of here tonight."

Winnie Ruth scratched her cheek lightly. "Can do, Frora-san, but the scurr is rocked up in the boathouse. And Mad Myrtre keeps the keys, rocked in her desk. And she won't reave that desk when she's got her pipe, her srippers and her fidrrers three." Then she emitted a slow hiss as her eyes lit up in triumph. "There is another way. The way I tried to go before you, Frora-san, and you, Fauna-san, came here. I got caught then, but tonight, everyone eat too much and drink too much and are protzed! Yes!" "S" hissed its way around the cell like a flying serpent. She jumped to her feet, crossed to her foot locker, opened it, extracted a cardboard sign and handed it to Flora. "Hang this on the door."

The sign read "Do Not Disturb." Flora followed the order and shut the door.

Winnie Ruth rubbed her hands together glee-fully, then moved to the mat at the center of the cell. She pulled the mat back, then tugged with her fingers at a large square of cement block that had obviously been cut into the floor with a blunt instrument.

"Herp me!" she whispered to Flora.

Flora knelt at the opposite side of the cement square and with one gargantuan effort pulled it loose, revealing a gaping hole.

"*Voirà!*" cried Winnie Ruth exaltedly. "I dug it arr out myserf. Secret tunner to freedom! Give me my rose and my grove and ret's go!"

"They'll send the bloodhounds after us!" exclaimed the terrified Fauna.

Flora rewarded her fear with a disdainful snap of her fingers. "So what? In our time we've had worse than noisy mutts nipping at our rears. Get our gear together, baby, it's the marines to the rescue!"

⋘§⋙

"No Chichevache will make a meal of *me*," chortled Ruthelma between bites of a nougat. She was perched on the edge of the back seat of a gypsy taxicab she had commandeered by phone an hour earlier. Her chauffeur, an unpublished poet of sillographs, which, he had carefully explained, were satirical poems few editors found amusing and what the hell did *they* know, wondered what the hell she was talking about. Ever since he had pulled "sillographs" on her, Ruthelma had been searching for a topper, and she munched content-edly with the realization she had pulled one.

"Chichevaches," she began explaining blithely, "were medieval *monsters* reputed to have *fed* on patient *wives*, and as a *result* were terribly *undernourished*." She wolfed another chunk of nougat and looked out the window at the two buildings across the street, returning to the vigil she had been keeping for well over half an hour. Her eagle eyes had already received a bonus. She had seen a pretty blond girl carrying a suitcase slip out of the basement of the Tara Club, run toward a parked Volkswagen, slip a key into the door, get in behind the wheel and drive off with a mean screeching of rubber on pavements. She had recognized Beth Alcott, and *tingled*.

"Are you a private eye, lady?" asked the chauffeur, whose name was Felix and who was lately wondering whether or not to readmit himself to the narcotics institute in Lexington.

"Heavens, *no*," replied Ruthelma, now daintily licking the tips of the five fingers of her right hand, "I'm an *impatient* wife and *literary* agent."

Felix almost jumped into the back seat with her. "Do you handle any poets?" he asked eagerly.

"*Never*." It hit him like the flat of a hand on the top of his head. "*Slim* volumes make for *slim* commissions. And I don't *understand* poetry *these* days. It's all *rhyme* without *reason*, and the *Kaufmann* Auditorium can *have* it."

Her eyes were glued to the windows on the second floor above the Tara Club. *What's* going *on* up there? Are they *bearding* the *lioness* in her *den*? Or are they *helpless* houseflies in the *parlor* of that awful *arachnid*? You're a *spider*, Topsy Alcott. A *mean* and *evil* and *vicious* black-widow *spider*. But *you'll* be *fooled*. Those *houseflies* you've welcomed are *exterminators* in *disguise*. And if those *exterminators* aren't out of there in *ten* minutes, I'm going to *crash*.

◈

Mr. Rachel would look back on the cocktail party and its participants as something more mercurial and fabulous than any sequence in *Alice in Wonderland*. From the moment Ocelot had entered, a strange if uneasy truce reigned. If Ocelot still nurtured doubts of her ability to take over and hold an audience, she could now dispel them with the self-assurance of Ursula Andress buying a D-cup brassiere. In less than a minute, she had twitted Topsy into the abatement of her anger and the rescinding of her orders for the assemblage to disperse. Topsy recognized the meaningful look in Ocelot's cat eyes and begrudgingly permitted her to take over. Ocelot swiftly wove a magic spell over Madeleine and her escorts.

And most intrigued of all was Satan Stagg. Ocelot seemed to favor commanding his attention each time she reached the point of an anecdote, as though they shared a tacit affinity. It recalled those weeks when he first made detective and Pharaoh Love had more or less adopted him by mutual though unspoken agreement. "*We are Toussaint L'Ouverture and Dessalines, cat*." And what are *we*, Ocelot? Duke Ellington and Josephine Baker? And what's with Madeleine and Peter and Robert? Madeleine's another woman, so I can understand the way she's examining Ocelot like an opal under a loupe. But what's that expression on Robert's face? I know it well. I saw it several times last night at Ida's Place when anything Topsy said triggered a suspicion in his head. And look at Peter. I don't understand that sly look at all. It's more catlike than Ocelot's, though most of her face is hidden behind that beautifully designed mask.

"It's really something to be a protégée of Topsy's," purred Ocelot. "Those ingenious little cities she booked me into at first. My dears, until I played them I'm sure they were known only to missionaries. Clayville and Portsburg and Stamplet. Thank *God* for Baltimore." Satan saw that Topsy was fidgeting. "I played Baltimore *four* times in six months. They couldn't get enough of me. Dear me, I seem to be monopolizing the conversation!"

Igor, having cleaned up the previous mess he'd made, passed among them with a new tray of hot hors d'oeuvres. The pain in his neck was now excruciating, and he fought to keep his face neutral. And he was fascinated. He was fascinated by the sudden calm that had overtaken the previously roiling atmosphere. But who had told the intruders of his relationship to Zoltan and Guru? That could mean the end of Igor. And Igor has no intention of hanging around to find out. Beth escaped. Igor can escape. The way Topsy looks at me. The way Ocelot looks at me. Don't the others see it? Are they blind to the eyes of murder? If I could slip out to the garden, through the gate next door and demand Zoltan's protection.

Protect me, Uncle, or the walls shall speak.

Clayville and Baltimore and Portsburg and Baltimore and Stamplet and Baltimore. Robert had run the names over and over again in his mind and had finally consigned them to memory. Keep talking, egotistical cat-lady. Keep talking. I'm a master at listening between the lines. My ego is as gargantuanly monumental. Keep talking. I'm already nursing a very important and very strong suspicion about where you fit in this jigsaw puzzle. You're far from the red herring you appeared to be at first. The way George S. Kaufman had a genius for whittling each act of a comedy down to its bare essentials, so am I whittling away at your run-on sentences. And I'm right, because Topsy is fidgeting. Topsy is nervous. Meg and Amy are nervous. If Topsy doesn't control those fingers, that string of pearls will break, sending those priceless baubles scattering across the rug, the way Ocelot's priceless baubles are scattering into my ears. Peter. Satan. Madeleine. Mr. Rachel. Am I coming through? Are my thought waves reaching you?

"Does 'Rosebud' mean anything to you?" Robert heard himself saying.

Ocelot's eyes flashed a warning to Topsy, who seemed about to leap from her chair.

" 'Rosebud'? Where'd *that* suddenly come from?"

"It was the last word spoken by Guru Raskalnikov before he died."

"Don't drop that tray!" Topsy shouted to Igor, and he retrieved it in time to avoid another disaster.

187

"I didn't know the gentleman," said Ocelot with a piquant smile.

Robert's smile matched hers. "I'll bet you did."

"And when would that have been?"

"In another world."

Ocelot stirred her scotch and water with an index talon.

"The world you lived in before you became Ocelot. What's your real name?"

"Call me Ishmael."

"Ishmael what?" asked Madeleine innocently, desperate for an appropriate moment to make her excuses and return to Zoltan. She'd been gone almost an hour, and she'd promised Arkie after one drink she'd be back. But Ocelot had been holding her hypnotized. I know that woman. Somewhere we've met before. Was she one of my supporting players in *Congo Circe*, the musical based on Stanley's search for Livingstone? Or perhaps it was in Paris at Gordon Heath's club. I've locked horns with this one before.

Ocelot ignored Madeleine's query and concentrated on Robert. "Ocelot is Ocelot, the way Hildegarde is Hildegarde and Fernandel is Fernandel. Ocelot belongs to herself. She shares only her unique and highly individualistic talents. From what I've read of him, and I do a great deal of reading, the late Raskalnikov struck me equally as unique and individual. I think Rosebud was his private joke."

"Any bets?" It was Peter who made the offer.

This is all so unreal and so bizarre, thought Mr. Rachel to himself. I've stumbled into a surrealist's nightmare. Not even Jameson Hurst and that insane fantasy that passed for his life could match this. I want to leave, but some invisible magnet whose strength far outweighs my fragile bones keeps me locked in this chair. Don't the others sense the danger? I can't give the danger a name, but I can sense it. I can feel it. These people we're dealing with are no longer rational. We're enjoying (*enjoying!*) the hospitality of maniacs. Topsy is mad. Her daughters are mad. And this *Ocelot!* The way she looks at Satan Stagg. Like the cat about to devour the canary. Or is it another kind of hunger? Oh, Ruthelma, Ruthelma. Forgive me. Forgive me. I know not what I have done.

"I'm a gambling woman," Rachel heard Ocelot say to Peter, "but at the moment all my chips are on Ocelot. I'm not interested in Raskalnikov or his murder. That's the past. My eyes are on tomorrow. Are you all coming to my opening Wednesday night?"

Beth headed the Volks up the Taconic State Parkway toward Albany.

Oh, please, Albany. Be the right direction for Canada. And, holy petroleum, I'm almost out of gas. I'll stop at the next filling station and—holy getaway, I can ask for a road map! I hope they haven't missed me yet. I've had an hour's head start. So what if they do miss me? They'll never guess which direction I've taken. But damn it. Topsy's smart. She'll figure Igor had something to do with this. But I didn't tell Igor where I was going! I'm safe! I'm safe! I'm safe!

❧

The three fugitives crawled rapidly through the underbrush that abutted the parkway.

"Flora," gasped Fauna, "let's stop for a minute and rest. My knees are sore and my hands are bleeding."

"There's a culvert up ahead," said Flora. "Let's make for it. We can rest there."

"A curvert?"

"Don't ask questions, Winnie Ruth. Just follow me."

"I'm forrowing, Frora-san."

Three minutes later they sat against the cool rock wall of the culvert, dangling their bruised hands in the small stream that flowed through it.

"Thank God they didn't send the dogs after us," said Fauna.

"What dogs?" asked Winnie Ruth. "They got no more brood hounds back there. That Riry Rarakurarai from Hawaii eat em arr. Baked dog Hawaiian dericacy. I hear Mad Myrtre terr her months ago, 'Sure, Riry, herp yourserf. We can use the kenners for a handbarr court!'"

Flora sat back and lit a cigarette. "We have to make better time. At the rate we're going, we'll never make New York by midnight."

"Ret's stear a car."

"Steal a car! Say," cried Flora, slapping an ample thigh, "that's a great idea! But where do we find one with the keys in it?"

"Easy," said Winnie Ruth confidently. "Firring station. I'rr go reconnoiter and find firring station." And silently she slipped away.

"That Winnie Ruth's a gem," said Flora, putting an arm around Fauna and patting her gently. "Without her, we'd have never made it."

Fauna rested her head on Flora's shoulder. "Flora, supposing we're too late. Supposing . . ."

"Don't think about it, baby," urged Flora. "If anything happens to Madeleine and the boys, that bitch Topsy'll answer to me. The way Sweet Harriet did." She chuckled. "And she, so to speak, got hoist by her own petard. Rest, baby, we got a long haul ahead of us."

❧

Guru's room? Is this Guru's room? What am I doing here?

Almighty Zeus. Have I suffered my second blackout? There's no time to waste. No time to waste. I must hurry. I must finish this before the others return.

Why did I come to Guru's room?

Of course. I remember. I remember.

He reached for the table and with an effort pulled himself to his feet. Paper. There's lots of paper here. Good. Good.

I must silence the walls.

❧

Ada clutched the weeping Jo to her bosom.

"Oh, God, miracles do happen. Thank you, dear Lord, thank you! Jo, Jo. You'll be safe. Ada will see to that. The twins are downstairs with the detective. I'll go down and get them."

Jo pulled back with terror in her eyes.

"There's nothing to be afraid of! Those three are a match for Topsy and that—that disgusting *Ocelot*. I'll go down there and tell them what you've told me. Think of it, just think of it—what they've been looking for has been right in this house all along. Right in the closet. You poor sweet darling. All this time in fear of your life and afraid to tell me. If you had only trusted me sooner. We could have had you out of here and in a good hospital where you belong. But just think of it. Working on yourself. Working all this time without even Ada guessing. Working to get feeling back in your fingers and getting that fog out of your head. Oh, Jo, Jo. I'm so proud of you. So proud. Now, you sit here. I'm going to lock the door from the outside. Don't be frightened. Everything's going to be just fine now. It's the end of Topsy and you're free. *Free*. Just think of it. The nightmare's over."

She wriggled her nostrils.

"What the hell's that cockeyed chef up to now? Can't he smell that dinner burning?"

"I think it's time everyone left. I'm a bit tired, and, Ocelot, you need your rest, too." The words spoken to Ocelot were delivered with special significance. "I'll have Igor show you to the door. Igor? Igor? Meg, Amy. Get Igor."

Mr. Rachel bounced to his feet in energetic relief. It most certainly *is* time to go. It was time to go forty minutes ago as far as I'm concerned.

Satan started to cross toward Ocelot, but, sensing his approach, she lithely turned and headed for the staircase.

"Good night," said Satan to the retreating figure. Ocelot waved a taloned hand in response.

Madeleine crossed to Peter and Robert and stood between them. Peter was staring at Ocelot, who seemed to have frozen in position at the foot of the stairs.

Ada Bergheim was descending into the room.

"Good heavens!" cried Peter. "Look who's here, Robert. It's Ada Bergheim. Ben Bentley's sister." Peter smiled at Topsy. "Miss Bergheim was more than cooperative in helping us with our research for *In Cold Water*. Quite contrary, I might say, to the reticent attitude of this household."

Topsy crossed to meet Ada. "How dare you leave Jo alone in her room?"

Jo, thought Robert. Good grief. We never had a chance to get to her.

Ada stared right past Topsy bravely. "Mr. Stagg, Miss Alcott would like to see you and the Moulin brothers immediately."

The blood drained from Topsy's face. Meg clutched Amy's arm, and Amy howled as the gesture caused her to stick herself with a pin. Ocelot's grip tightened on the handrail, and Mr. Rachel hoped there was someone to catch him when he fainted. As though the choreography had been rehearsed for weeks, Peter, Robert and Satan moved in unison toward Ada.

Topsy stepped ahead of them swiftly and barred their way.

"You make one move up that staircase and I shall send for the police!"

"My good woman," said Satan coolly, "the police are here."

&⊰⊱&

"*Goodness!*" cried Ruthelma. "What's *daylight* doing here at *this* hour?"

The chauffeur was staring out the windshield at the Zoltan mansion. "That isn't daylight, sweetheart. There's a house on fire."

"A *house* on *fire!*" Ruthelma pressed her nose against the window and saw flames shooting out from the rear of the mansion. "Oh, my *God!* Quick! *Run* to the corner and *send* the *alarm!*"

She struggled out of the car as Felix got out of the front and sprinted toward the fire alarm box. Ruthelma waddled across the street and banged on the front door of the Zoltan mansion.

"*Fire!* Fire! *Fire!*"

&⊰⊱&

Jo clutched the arms of her chair in terror.

Smoke! The house is on fire!

The smoke was pouring through the partially opened windows into the room.

I want to scream. I want to scream. But I can't. I can't.

"*Urgle gurgle urgle gurgle.*"

With an effort, she began rocking the chair back and forth until it tipped forward and she plunged face downward to the floor. Slowly, she began crawling toward the closet.

Rosebud. I must save Rosebud.

"R-r-ro-o-s-se-b-b-uh-uh-uh-dddd."

Who said that?

Me. It was *me*. I can *talk*.

Hurry back, Ada. Hurry back. I can talk. *I can talk*.

I'm coming, Rosebud, *I'm coming*.

<svg> ❧ </svg>

"*Fire!*" shrieked Ruthelma to the footman who answered the door. "Your house is on *fire!*"

The footman shrieked, "Mary!" and rushed past Ruthelma into the street.

Ruthelma bravely rushed into the entrance hall.

"Mr. *Zoltan!*" she cried as the fumes, the smoke and the choking acridity began tearing at her lungs. "Mr. *Zoltan!*"

Two footmen rushed to the second floor the back way, but the flames had already reached there and forced them back. Another footman pulled the chain to the fire system, and the clamor of bells reverberated through the mansion and were heard by the occupants of Topsy's duplex.

"The fire alarm!" cried Topsy. "Next door! *Zoltan!*"

"*Zoltan!*" Madeleine bolted toward the stairway that led to the street.

"Smoke!" cried Ada. "The upper floor is filled with smoke! The fire's spreading here! Jo! Jo!"

Ocelot roughly shoved Ada aside and bolted up the stairs with Satan, Peter and Robert in pursuit.

Amy turned to Meg. "Let's get out of here."

In Topsy's garden, Igor stared with horror at the flames shooting from Guru's bedroom.

Trapped! I am trapped! He scurried back into the basement of the Tara Club.

Madeleine dashed up the stairs and into the Zoltan mansion. She fought her way through the black curtain of smoke to the stairs.

"Mr. *Zoltan*, where *are* you?" she heard Ruthelma yelling from the staircase.

"Ruthelma!" Cough cough cough. "Ruthelma, where are you? It's *me*. Madeleine Cartier!"

"I'm in the *middle* of the *staircase* and I can't *see* a *thing!*" Madeleine heard her through the shrill cacophony of the fire bells and fought her way to her side.

"Arkie!" Cough cough cough. "We have to save Arkie! Where are those dizzy footmen?"

"They *lammed!*"

"Look. Look—at the head of the stairs. Arkie! Arkie! We're coming!" Cough cough cough. "We're coming!"

Zoltan clutched the handrail to steady himself.

The third blackout. This is it. The count is almost over. This is it. He mustered his remaining strength and plowed it all into a piccolo coda.

"Go back, Madeleine!" he tweetled. "Go back! It's too late for me! Too late!"

Tears were streaming down Ruthelma's face, and her chest felt stickily damp. With a groan she realized two chocolate bars in her pocket were melting.

And then she heard Madeleine shrieking. The

sound was piercingly hideous, and it would ring in Ruthelma's ears on occasion in months to come. It was an eternal shreik that never seemed to end until Ruthelma reached Madeleine's side and stared down at Zoltan, who had crumpled to the floor.

"Oh, my *God!*" cried Ruthelma. "Oh, my *God!* He . . . he . . . Oh, my *God!* He's—*disintegrating!*"

She grabbed Madeleine to keep her from falling backward down the stairs and propped her against the banister.

Madeleine repeated over and over again, oblivious to Ruthelma's chubby hands rapidly slapping her cheeks to bring her out of her hysteria:

"Hideous   hideous   hideous   hideous   *hideous* . . ."

12

THE GAS STATION attendant struggled to loosen the gag in his mouth and the rope that bound his hands and feet securely. That big broad sure knows how to tie a knot, he thought to himself ruefully. Overpowered by three women. Well, I never. And the way that Jap came at me with the karate chop, yelling *"Banzai!"* I'll never live this one down. Never. I'll move the family to Larchmont. You can really get lost in Larchmont.

❧

Winnie Ruth bore down on the gas and the horn as she steered the car kamikaze style toward New York.

"Careful," whimpered the terrified Fauna in the front seat next to her, "that was an oil truck you almost sideswiped."

Winnie Ruth chortled gleefully. "Screw oir

trucks. I rike driving cars. Never drove in my rife!"

In the back seat, Beth beat her fists against Flora's solid chest, looking like Mae Marsh fending off her would-be rapist in *The Birth of a Nation*.

Flora lost patience with the ineffectual massage and shoved Beth away.

"Cut the athletics, blondie, and relax. We're desperate women."

"So am I," howled Beth. "I don't want to go back to New York. Topsy'll kill me!"

Winnie Ruth swerved to avoid hitting a station wagon, and Flora and Fauna stared at Beth.

"Topsy?" bellowed Flora. "Topsy *Alcott?*"

Beth nodded as she fumbled in her purse for a handkerchief.

"That's the broad *we're* after, kid!"

Beth's head shot up.

"You heard of Madeleine Cartier and the Moulin twins?"

Beth nodded dumbly.

"That's my daughter and my grandsons! They're in danger. Fauna here, Madeleine's sister—no baby, not the one that's driving, this one—saw it all in her crystal ball. Well, what a stroke of luck!" She clapped her ham-hock hand on Beth's fragile back. "This kid can lead us straight to Madeleine and the boys! What's Topsy got it into *you* for?"

Beth sniffled. "I may as well tell you all of it. I'm doomed anyway. Holy psychopathic, wait'll you hear *this*."

❧

"Not since . . ." cough cough cough, "Margo left . . ." cough cough cough, "Shangri La . . ." cough cough cough, "have I seen anything as horrible . . ." cough cough cough, "as this. Are his legs too heavy?"

"I'm *managing*," gasped Ruthelma as she and Madeleine lugged Zoltan down the staircase. In the distance they heard the comforting wailing of fire engine sirens. Madeleine renewed her grip on Zoltan's shoulders, averting her eyes from his face.

The skin was no longer alabaster. It had shriveled into mummylike parchment. His leonine mane had turned oyster white, and his lips were as shriveled as raisins. His fingers had twisted into gnarled little twigs, and the body seemed to have shrunk to a third of its size.

Perhaps we should have left him on the landing. Better cremation than this. But no. No. That would be inhuman. What's that terrible brown stain on Ruthelma's blouse?

"His *lips* are *moving*," cried Ruthelma as they gently lowered him to the floor at the foot of the stairs. "He's *trying* to say something."

Madeleine choked back a sob as Ruthelma bravely lowered her head and placed her left ear to Zoltan's shriveled mouth.

❧

Jo crawled from the closet toward the door. The room was a deadly black fog of smoke, and she felt her strength ebbing.

The door. I've got to make the door. Where is Ada? Why hasn't she come for me? The door. I've got to— Oh, God! It's locked from the outside. Ada! Ada, where are you? Ada!

◆§◈◈

On the staircase leading to the top landing, Ada shrieked, "Look out!" and pressed tightly against the wall as Satan grabbed Peter and Robert by their jackets and pulled them to one side. The marble statue Ocelot had hurled at them sailed past their heads and crashed against the wall. Ocelot rushed toward Jo's door and with a superhuman display of strength crashed against it.

I've got to get to her. I've got to get to her before *they* do. I don't want to do it, Jo baby, I don't. But I have to. I have to.

She crashed against the door again, and the panel splintered.

Stinking fire. Stinking holocaust. Who set it? Who did this to me? I had it made, damn it! I had it made! Did Topsy arrange it? Was it another one of her cute little tricks? They're closing in on us, she'd screamed. They're closing in on us. Let's get out now. Women. Stupid hysterical women. Strong Topsy. Clever Topsy. Formidable Topsy. A tower of Jell-O.

Another panel splintered as an alien arm coiled around her neck in a viselike grip. I know that one, baby. I can handle that one easy.

Ocelot feigned limpness and then, as the arm relaxed, brutally shot her right elbow into Satan's groin. The detective grunted and fell back, hands covering his face as five razor-sharp talons cut through the cloth of his sleeve. Ocelot's foot shot out and caught Satan in his chest, propelling him back against the approaching twins, and the three fell to the floor in a tangled heap.

Now I get her, then out the back window down the drainpipe, into the garden and out. The place'll be swarming with firemen and fuzz, and I've got to move fast. Topsy better be waiting for me at Checkpoint Charlie. She'd just better be waiting for me.

Ada felt five skinny fingers clutching at her wrist. Through the swirling smoke, she discerned Mr. Rachel's features.

He managed to choke out, "Where's the back staircase?"

Ada grabbed his hand and led the way.

The twins scrambled to their feet and helped Satan to his. There was no more than an inch of visibility on the top landing, but they heard Jo's door splinter again and then give way, and the three groped their way in the direction of the ominous sound.

Outside, the flames leaped from the Zoltan mansion to the adjoining building, and the crowd gathered in the street emitted a roar.

A hook-and-ladder engine maneuvered the turn into the street, and somebody yelled, "Who's that hanging on the back?"

"The Mayor."

～§§～

Igor huddled under the blanket in the back seat of the Citroen. Garage door locked. Everything locked. Igor will be safe here from the flames. The garage is all cement, Topsy had it constructed like a vault. Topsy hides everything here. Igor will be safe.

Then he heard the whirring of the motor that controlled the garage door. Then the clatter of high heels. Then the opening of the front door. The insertion of the key and the ignition. Then the car jerked and took off, and Igor groaned inwardly.

Igor going for a ride.

Topsy directed the car out of the underground garage into the street and swerved left, narrowly missing a head-on collision with a police car coming at her from the opposite direction. Part of the crowd screamed and moved back as the Citroen hit a fire plug, tearing it loose and sending a geyser of water into the air.

Three drenched young men linked arms and sang at the top of their lungs, "San Francisco-o-o-o-o, open your golden gates . . ."

The Zoltan mansion was news and the Tara Club was news, and word of the fire spread to radio and television fifteen minutes after the alarm had been raised.

Veronica's ears quivered and her face paled as the news emanated from the lonesome bartender's transistor radio. She opened her purse, extracted a bill, slapped it on the counter and, coatless, dashed from the bar into the lobby of her hotel, through the revolving doors and out into the street, screaming "Cab! Cab! Cab!" One of these days, one of these days very soon, she muttered to herself in a rage, I'm going to roam the streets with a bag of rocks and use those stinking "Off Duty" blinkers for target practice.

Ida got her information from CBS's Jim Jensen, for whom she harbored a secret passion. She was off the bed and into her trenchcoat in two minutes flat. She grabbed her purse, ran into the hall, pressed the down button for an elevator and, after five minutes of waiting, began pounding at the elevator door and sent the two maiden ladies in an adjoining apartment scurrying under their beds.

❧

At first Jo couldn't see who it was who came crashing through the door. It couldn't be Ada, she knew. Ada has a key. Ada can let herself in. Ada wouldn't have the strength to break the door down. Her fingers tightened on the object she had taken from the closet. Though the room was black with smoke, she had seen the flames licking at the windows, and with terror in her heart she knew they'd soon bleed their way into the room.

"Kitten . . . kitten . . ." She heard the all-too-familiar voice. "Where are you, kitten?"

She cringed against the sideboard and prayed not to lose her balance.

Where are the others? She pleaded inwardly to a deaf God. Where's the detective and the twins?

Robert staggered to the doorway and groped his way into the room. Someone was behind him, but he couldn't be sure if it was Peter or Satan. Downstairs he could hear windows crashing and the sound of axes against wood.

Don't firemen ever use doorknobs? wondered Mr. Rachel as Ada led him up the back stairs to the top floor. And of what use will either one of us be after we reach our destination? If Satan and the twins can't rescue the girl, what use will a woman and a fragile caterer be? Ada's grip tightened on his wrist and he decided Ada might be of some use after all.

"Wow!" cried a spectator to Felix the chauffeur. "Just like *In Old Chicago!*"

Felix wondered if the spectator could feel his talented fingers lifting his wallet.

A sweet-faced creature turned into the gawking face of a handsome young man and innocently inquired, "Do you come here often?"

Veronica was elbowing her way with utmost difficulty through the crowd. She roughly jabbed a woman to one side, and the woman, hand half raised to strike back, suddenly growled instead, "Hullo, baby. Long time no see."

Veronica cringed inwardly. "Oh—hello, Audrey." Her partner in an incriminating photo the late Ben Bentley had used for blackmail.

"Good show," said Audrey, indicating the holocaust with a brusque wave of her hand, "I'd like to get the musical rights," which she punctuated with a grim guffaw.

"Excuse me," said Veronica hastily, "I've got to get through. I've got friends in there."

"In *there!*" snorted Audrey. "They must be *fried.*"

From another direction, Ida wedged her way

toward the police cordon. There was a frantic look on her face. The twins. Madeleine. And God knows who else.

"Any survivors?" she gasped to a policeman.

He nodded. "Yeah, these two." He pointed to Amy and Meg.

Meg clutched at Ida's arm. "You got any cash on you? We couldn't save a thing. Please, Ida. Give us what you got."

"The back of my hand," snarled Ida, pulling her arm away.

Amy started to menace her with a pin.

"You know where you can stick *that!*" yelled Ida as she slapped the pin out of Amy's hand.

A cry rose from the crowd.

Madeleine and Ruthelma were emerging from the mansion assisted by two firemen, followed by another fireman with Zoltan slung over his back. He carried the shrunken body to a waiting ambulance.

"Thank you, thank you," gasped Madeleine as Ruthelma sank to the curb gasping for air, "you have rescued . . . Madeleine Cartier."

Hysterical, decided the fireman. I know Shirley Temple when I see her.

"Madeleine! Madeleine!" screeched **Veronica**. "What happened to *Zoltan?*"

Madeleine had difficulty focusing her eyes, but her ears were in excellent shape. She now had her arms around the well-built, handsome young fireman's neck, her head against his chest as her body convulsed with sobs.

"Madeleine! Madeleine!"

Ruthelma looked up wearily. "It's *Veronica*." She pronounced the name like a doctor informing a patient it's leprosy.

Ida shoved two policemen aside and rushed to Ruthelma and Madeleine.

"The boys!" she yelled. "Where are the boys?"

Madeleine suddenly snapped to attention.

"My babies!" she shrieked. "Save my babies!"

"Babies!" gasped a woman in the crowd. "That woman's babies are in one of those burning buildings!"

It spread like wildfire, and the crowd took up the chant. "Save the babies! Save the babies!"

The Mayor tore himself away from the three television cameras that had been rushed to the scene and shouted, "Save those babies!"

"Who's he?" asked a very old lady in a very old and quivering voice.

"The Mayor," someone told her.

The old lady squinted her eyes. "He don't look like La Guardia."

◂§▸

The razor talons flashed before Jo's smoke-filled eyes. She screamed and the object she had been holding crashed to the floor. Satan's ears guided him toward the scream as Peter steadied Robert, who was on the verge of collapsing. Ocelot lunged at Jo, who in swerving to avoid the deadly talons lost her balance and fell to the floor. Satan's flying tackle hit its target. Talons slashed at his face as Satan drove a fist into a cat eye. Ocelot shoved Satan aside and leaped to her feet, crouching, waiting to spring with talons poised to rip. Peter rushed to Satan's aid and then felt himself plummeting headlong to the floor as he tripped over the object Jo had dropped. Satan sailed into Ocelot with his right fist, and, though Ocelot swerved, the fist caught her shoulder and she fell backward.

In the hallway, Ada fought her way through the smoky blackness toward Jo's room.

"Ada! Ada!" Mr. Rachel yelped between choking coughs as he groped his way along the wall. This, he decided, is utterly ridiculous. I'll never hear the last of it from Ruthelma.

✧⁂✧

Igor is trapped!

His neck ached mercilessly as his head kept hitting the floor of the car. If she knows I'm crouched on the floor of the back seat under this blanket, she'll kill me.

Guru. Guru. You should have listened to me. You should have obeyed your father's counsel. Who lives with evil dies of evil. Old Transylvanian proverb, and the old proverbs are still the best.

She must have gone through dozens of red lights. I can hear motorcycle sirens. And what else is that I hear? She's singing! She is mad! Completely mad! At a time like this, she is singing!

The speedometer of the Citroen read a precarious hundred and ten, and at the top of her lungs Topsy bellowed, "There'll be some changes made!" Her hands on the wheel were reality. Her foot pressing the pedal to the floorboard was reality. The sound of pursuing motorcycles was reality.

This icy parkway heading north was reality. The car swerving from side to side was reality.

But in her mind Topsy dwelt on fantasy. Everything up in flames, but, like the phoenix, Topsy is newly arisen. So what if one world slipped through Topsy's fingers? Topsy can buy herself another world. The strongbox is on the seat next to Topsy, and it contains millions in hoarded cash and jewelry. Topsy will make it over the border into Canada, hop a plane from Montreal to London, and Tara will rise again somewhere in Mayfair.

Why did Topsy run? Why did Topsy panic? Couldn't Topsy have brazened it through? There were only two pieces of evidence to align Topsy with Guru's murder. The wallpaper and Rosebud. But the wallpaper must have been obliterated by the flames. Zoltan must have seen to that. That fire was no accident. Topsy knows arson, because Topsy's set many a fire of her own in her time. Zoltan must have done it. Zoltan didn't come for cocktails. Zoltan wasn't well, she'd seen that in Madeleine's troubled face. That idiot Goldberg. Never did know how to judge a dose. The blackouts must have begun, and Zoltan's no fool. He knew the score. Zoltan.

"I loved you, Zoltan!" shrieked Topsy in a harpy's voice, and Igor trembled beneath the blanket.

"I loved you, you ancient bastard! I should have been your empress!"

Topsy turned on the windshield wiper, but too late realized the blur was her own tear-filled eyes. Confusion overpowered her brain and she lost control of the wheel. She fought to regain it as the motorcycle sirens screamed closer and closer, and she could feel the Citroen plow through the protective railing and saw the Volks hurtling toward her from the opposite direction, and Topsy screamed.

"Fasten your seat berts!" yelled Winnie Ruth Judo, twisting the wheel desperately to avert a head-on crash as the Citroen came hurtling toward them. Fauna shrieked and covered her face with her hands. Flora angrily smacked Winnie Ruth on the back of her head. Beth cried, "Holy smackup!" and then the cars collided.

The Citroen hit the right front of the Volks as Winnie Ruth veered in an attempt to avoid it. The Citroen skidded and hit a cement abutment with an agonizing force that sent it rolling over and hurling down an embankment. The Volks began spinning as Winnie Ruth bravely fought to keep it from overturning. Flora smacked her three more times on the back of the head and then hit her own head on the roof of the car as it bounced against the guard rail and came to a stop. Flora fell on top of Beth, who mercifully had blacked out, and the sound of Fauna's whimpering told Flora her offspring was still among the living. Winnie Ruth's head had fallen against the horn, which emitted an ugly blare. Flora reached forward, grabbed Winnie Ruth's head by the hair and pulled it back.

"Baby, Barney Oldfield you ain't!"

"My babies! My babies! My babies!" shrieked Madeleine as the television cameras were trained in her direction.

Ruthelma held tightly to Ida's firm hand. "*My* Rachel! My *Rachel!*"

Veronica added to the flames by applying a cigarette lighter to a Marlboro and then realized she was freezing. She shook her head sadly. Up in flames. Everything up in flames.

"Miss Cartier!" shouted one of the cameramen. "Could you face a little more to the left, please?"

"My babies! My babies!" cried Madeleine as she faced a little more to the left.

❦

That cat's a tiger, thought Peter, his jaw in agony. Ocelot leaped around the room with stunning feline grace as she tried to work her way toward the window.

Jo was crumpled in a heap on the floor. Ada had found her way to her side and tried to call her name, but all she could do was gag. Anger surged through her body as her right hand made contact with the object Jo had dropped.

At the same time, Satan's right fist made contact with Ocelot's face and the cat-woman stumbled backward, tripped and fell at Ada's feet.

Bitch. Evil Bitch, thought Ada. Evil evil bitch. She took a firm grip on the object and raised it above her head as Mr. Rachel came stumbling into the room.

Ocelot twisted her head and groggily stared up

at the object in Ada's hands descending toward her skull. The cat eyes widened in horror, the cat mouth opened, and from it emerged in a shriek:

"Rosebud!"

13

AMBULANCES and two police cars were rushing to the scene of the highway crash.

One of the motorcycle policemen stared with revulsion at Topsy's body, which had gone through the windshield. A second policeman pulled Igor from the rear of the wreckage, gulped and then said to the other, "This one's neck's broken."

Fauna held a handkerchief to her bleeding forehead, and Winnie Ruth sat on the ground wondering if it was possible to commit hara-kiri with a sliver of broken glass. Beth stood staring down at the smashed Citroen, struck dumb upon recognizing Topsy.

Flora was brazening it out with two other officers.

"Well, you see, us girls were late for a meeting."

She managed her most beguiling smile. "We're the local chapter of the B'nai B'rith."

"And what's your name?" asked one officer.

"I'm B'nai Venuta." She gently squeezed Fauna's shoulder, and Fauna winced.

"My erbow's busted," moaned Winnie Ruth.

"Sayyyy," said one of the officers, "I know that one! She's Winnie Ruth Judo. Her and two of her buddies broke out of the powder-puff prison a couple of hours ago! What a haul!" Flora's shoulders sagged and Fauna burst into tears.

"Mad Myrtre'rr kirr us," offered Winnie Ruth.

"Topsy," whispered Beth. The two officers who had examined the wreckage were climbing up the embankment. One said to Beth, "You recognize the stiff?"

Beth nodded. "Topsy Alcott."

The officer whistled as Flora bellowed, "Topsy *Alcott!*"

Beth nodded and Fauna's face brightened. "Oh, Flora! We did it! We did it! We didn't fail Madeleine and the boys!"

"Well, I'll be damned," said Flora proudly as she crossed to Beth's side and stared down at Topsy's face. "She wasn't bad-looking, was she, kid?"

"She's looked better."

The officer who had removed Igor from the back seat felt his knees begin to buckle.

"What's wrong, Trahey?" asked another officer.

"Look!" said Trahey, pointing to Igor, who was struggling to his feet with his head at its normal sixty-degree angle. "His—his neck's broken, but—

but he's *alive*. . . ." Trahey's eyes rolled up, disappeared, and he crashed face forward onto the ground in a faint.

Beth was rushing down the embankment to Igor, crying, "Igor! Igor! You're safe! You're alive! But what were you doing with Topsy, for heaven's sake!"

Igor stared at Topsy's body and chuckled. "Igor'sssss neckkkkk wassss achinggggg alllll dayyyy. Omennnn offff deathththth. Butttt omennnnn forrrr Topsyyyyy. Igorrrrr immortallllll!"

᪥

There was an imposing parade of ambulances leaving the scene of the fire. One held Jo Alcott and Ada. Another carted Zoltan's body to the morgue. A third contained Ruthelma, cooing anxiously over Mr. Rachel, a victim of smoke poisoning. A fourth contained the unconscious Ocelot with her skull bashed in, accompanied by Satan Stagg. Felix the chauffeur, who had bellowed after Ruthelma for his fare, was commandeered by the twins, Madeleine, Ida and Veronica and ordered to follow Ocelot's ambulance.

Meg and Amy stared ruefully at the charred shells that had once been the Zoltan mansion and Topsy's Tara.

"Whaht do we do now?" wondered Meg aloud.

"We'll go to Zelma the Zombie," said Amy. "She'll put us up till we're back on our feet again."

"We hahve no clothes except whaht we're wearing! Mr. Stahgg's wahrned us to be at the police stahtion first thing in the morning. Where cahn we get some clothes?"

"Zelma'll conjure some up."

❧§❧

The intern had removed the mask from Ocelot's face and was giving her emergency treatment. The clamor of the siren couldn't match the clamor in Satan's head. Rosebud. Ocelot. Zoltan. Murder. Raskalnikov.

Pharoah Love.

Ocelot stirred.

"I think she's coming to," said the intern as he wound bandages around Ocelot's head. The eyes fluttered open and fought to focus. Soon she recognized Satan. The lips moved and the voice struggled to articulate and after a few moments won the battle.

"Satan cat." There was even a trace of a smile. "You hear me?" Satan nodded. "Then listen good and listen carefully. I ain't making it to that hospital. I want you to have the scoop. Come closer. Can you hear me, Satan cat?"

"I can hear you, Pharoah."

❧§❧

Now it was midnight, the witching hour, and, like a coven of witches, they were huddled around a table at the rear of Ida's Place: Peter and Robert Moulin, Satan Stagg, Ida, Veronica, Madeleine Cartier, Ada Bergheim and Ruthelma Rachel. The jukebox was blissfully silent, and there were only six people at the bar to occupy the bartender's attention. There were occupants at only three of the other tables, and two waiters on duty struggled to keep from yawning. Ida was glad for this abnormally dull night at her place. It made it easier to concentrate on what was being said. Ruthelma had checked the hospital and been told Mr. Rachel was resting comfortably. Ada was confidant Jo was in good hands. The nightmare was over.

For some subconscious reason she would someday understand, Madeleine was drinking Sazeracs. They had heard hours ago the news of Topsy's death and of Flora, Fauna and Winnie Ruth's escape and recapture. I look like Shirley Temple, thought Madeleine to herself, and I feel like Marie Dressler.

"Start with Pharoah," Robert urged Satan. "Why the Ocelot masquerade?"

"It was no masquerade," said Satan, "it was the real thing. Why do you think the poor bugger spent so much time in Baltimore? He'd been in the hospital there for months. The constant rebookings at the Switch were for checkups and hormone shots. What was that song Pharoah kept humming, Ida?"

" 'There'll Be Some Changes Made.' "

"He made one," said Satan.

Ruthelma was goggle-eyed. "You mean like that Jorgenson boy . . . girl—whatever?"

"Topsy paid for it. It was part of the deal. Pharoah'd been with an analyst after Seth Piro's death. It led to his decision. But he didn't have the money to pay for the deal. And it takes a lot of money. He got chummy with Jo and Raskalnikov, and that brought him to Topsy. Topsy made a big play for Pharoah and he didn't discourage her. It was the one way he could get the money he needed. And Topsy had big problems of her own.

"She was planning to double-cross Zoltan. She had managed to get Raskalnikov to come in with her because he was nuts about Jo, wanted to marry her, but Zoltan forbade it. Igor got wind of the plot against Zoltan and warned Guru off. That's when Topsy tried to get him deported. But now Topsy was in over her head. Guru was backing out, and she knew sooner or later he or Igor or both would tip Zoltan.

"So Topsy hatched the plot to murder Raskalnikov and Igor."

"And *Igor*," said Ruthelma. "But Igor's still *alive*."

"All in good time, chubby one." Satan pinched her cheek, and Ruthelma giggled and bit into her Italian meatball hero sandwich. Robert's pencil raced across a page of his notebook.

"It wasn't *In Cold Water* that made Pharoah disappear four days before the murder. That was the way Topsy had planned it. She wanted Pharoah to make a mysterious disappearance because Guru and Igor were suspicious Topsy was out to get them through Pharoah. That's why Guru had come to see Pharoah the night before he pulled the vanishing act. To tell him not to try anything. That he'd get Pharoah first. Pharoah phoned Topsy, who then instructed him to come straight from this place to her duplex, where she kept him hidden until the night of the murder.

"Jo and the girls knew Pharoah was in the house. Jo slipped over to Guru's Christmas Eve to tip him. Guru, as Jo told me earlier, was prepared to take on Pharoah. You see, what Topsy didn't know was that Guru and Jo had been married in a secret ceremony earlier that week. So Jo took off her clothes and Rosebud . . ."

"What *is* Rosebud?" demanded Madeleine.

"In a minute," said Satan as Ada sipped her drink. "And Jo got into bed with Guru, who switched off the lights. Pharoah steals into the house with a key provided by Topsy, makes his way into Guru's room, planning to strangle him. He doesn't know Jo's there. He slips into the room and trips over Rosebud. Guru jumps up yelling, Jo's cowering under the bedcovers, Pharoah panics, picks up Rosebud and sends it crashing onto Guru's skull. Guru falls across Jo, who screams, and without looking to see who it is Pharoah brings Rosebud down on the bedcovers, hears the crack, figures the job's done, then switches on the lights and starts wiping his fingerprints off the weapon. Then he pulls back the covers, sees it's Jo and decides he needs help.

"He phones Topsy, who comes hustling over with Beth, Meg and Amy. They strap Rosebud back onto Jo, and Beth and Meg carry her out through the garden back to their place. Pharoah, Topsy and Amy stay behind to clean up the place. There's a quick discussion as to whether Igor should be knocked off, too, but now Topsy's against it. Guru dead is one thing. But Guru and Igor, that could set Uncle Zoltan thinking and doing some investigating of his own.

"Topsy's already got a dilly cooked up for Zoltan about how she found out Guru was planning to double-cross them and had to take matters into her own hands. Now, not knowing Guru still has that one breath left in him, they ring for Igor to establish the time of death, all of them having prepared alibis for each other, and get out of the place fast. Igor comes up a few minutes later from his room in the basement and finds Guru, whose dying word identifies the weapon. 'Rosebud.' "

He sipped his drink. "You tell them, Ada."

Ada cleared her throat. "Well, it seems Jo was in an automobile crash some years before she met Topsy. She lost a leg. Rosebud," she said primly, "was her artificial limb."

Peter brightened. "Rosebud Orthopedics!"

"Right," said Satan. "Jo's pet name for the limb was Rosebud."

"Goodness," murmured Ruthelma.

"Who *are* Jo and the girls?" asked Madeleine.

"Topsy's front," said Satan, "a clever cover devised for her by Zoltan. He needed to control four major monopolies in this country. What better way to get to them than through the four men at the top? So four girls were carefully screened, hired, paid fantastic salaries and trained to be Topsy's 'daughters.' Then the Tara Club was conceived. A fortune was spent for Topsy and her 'daughters' to make a big splash, and, just as Zoltan figured, all roads led to Tara and soon the four Johns he was after were well in the clutches of Meg, Beth, Amy and Jo. But nobody figured Jo would fall for Guru.

"Guru," he continued, "was an extension of Zoltan. Zoltan gave the orders, and he did the wheeling and dealing. This kept Zoltan free to operate in Europe and the Orient. And all of the operation was there in explicit detail on the wallpaper in Guru's room. What Topsy never knew but later suspected after Guru was dead was that Zoltan had designated Guru as his heir. If Topsy had controlled her greed a bit longer, she could have gotten what she wanted from Guru eventually."

"*Goodness*, boys, do you *realize*," rhapsodized Ruthelma to the twins, "what a *fantastic* book this'll *make?*"

"Why was Igor able to survive?" asked Peter.

"Igor never knew who murdered his son," explained Satan, "though he had his suspicions. He thought Jo had done it. That's why Topsy's strict orders to keep him away from her. Topsy let Igor continue blackmailing them because it was deductible. He was marked to get his, but Topsy wasn't about to do it herself. That was up to Pharoah, but he was undergoing his transition in Baltimore, so it had to wait. Topsy'd also been tipped by friend Goldberg in Switzerland that Zoltan's time was running out. Then along come you boys with plans to write the book, so events were closing in on Topsy. She had to move fast. Stop the book. Get rid of Igor. And work on Zoltan. But when she'd phoned Zoltan in Europe to go after Madeleine as one means of quashing the book, she didn't figure he'd propose marriage. So she had to move Ocelot into town sooner than she planned. Meantime, Jo, now a vegetable from the blow administered by Pharoah, is regaining her senses."

Ada explained in detail the blinking system she had patiently worked out with Jo. Satan resumed the narrative when Ada was finished.

"According to Jo, Ocelot came to her room and kissed her hand, and Topsy saw her wince when Ocelot's whiskers tickled her. Jo knew then she'd been added to Topsy's list, though Topsy'd been nuts about her."

"Now, why would four lovely girls accept the sort of proposition Topsy presented them?" Madeleine wondered aloud.

"For money and position," said Robert. "Why not? Girls do worse for less."

"*Some* girls," corrected Ada.

Madeleine turned to Ruthelma. "What did Zoltan whisper in your ear before he died?"

"Oh, *goodness!* I *almost* forgot *all* about *that*. Now, let me think. He said, 'Louis has will. The rest is lost forever. I love you, Shirley.'" She beamed at Madeleine. "I'm sure the *last* was meant for *you*."

Madeleine slammed the table with her hand. "I've come to a decision. I'm having my face redone."

Veronica stirred. "Well, there goes my publishing company." She thought for a moment, then said, "Say, Ruthelma. Isn't it about time you retired? How's about selling out to me?"

"*Never.*"

"To think," mused Ida, "I had the clue to Pharoah's disappearance all the time. No wonder that threat. I guess I just ain't as smart as I think I am."

"Holy *conspiracy!* I had an idea we'd find you here!" Beth came breezing into Ida's Place followed by Igor. "Have you heard? Topsy's dead! And say, listen!" She addressed the twins. "I met your grandmother and your aunt, and when you *really* get to know them they're darling!"

Beth and Igor now sat with the group.

"You should have heard them bellowing out the window of the squad car taking them back to the hoosegow. Some nutty song that went something like this: 'Tippy-tap-toe, tippy-tap-toe' something or another."

"Of all things. They must be mad," said Madeleine indignantly. "That was Sweet Harriet's song. Boys! We've got to get those two sprung!"

"Ida," sighed Robert wearily, "can we have another round of drinks?"

❧§❧

It was Wednesday, and a light snow was falling over the cemetery. A confused Baptist minister had finally consented to refer to the deceased as "Pharoah Love," though he'd been under the assumption the body in the coffin was a lady named Ocelot.

Ocelot is coming!

Satan smiled. Ida saw it out of the corner of her eye and wondered what he was thinking. Jo stood firmly on her right leg and Rosebud, holding Ada's hand. Madeleine sniffled into a black lace handkerchief, and the twins stood with their heads bowed. Mr. Rachel stood with his arm around Ruthelma, and at one moment, when her eyes met his, he tightened his grip and then regretted it when he heard two simultaneous crunching cracks, signifying the shattering of two hidden candy bars.

Ocelot is coming!

Satan watched the slowly descending coffin.

Ocelot is here.

GEORGE BAXT
His Life and Hard Times

On a Monday afternoon, June 11, 1923, George Baxt was born on a kitchen table in Brooklyn.

He was nine when his first published work appeared in the Brooklyn *Times-Union*. He received between two and five dollars for each little story or poem the paper used.

His first play was produced when he was eighteen. It lasted one night.

Mr. Baxt has been a propagandist for Voice of America, a press agent, and an actor's agent. He has written extensively for stage, screen, and television. During stays in England in the fifites, he wrote a number of films *(Circus of Horrors; Horror Hotel; Burn, Witch, Burn)* which are now staples of late night television.

His first novel, A QUEER KIND OF DEATH, was published in 1966. His other novels include SWING LOW, SWEET HARRIET; A PARADE OF COCKEYED CREATURES; TOPSY AND EVIL; "I!" SAID THE DEMON; PROCESS OF ELIMINATION; THE DOROTHY PARKER MURDER CASE; and most recently THE ALFRED HITCHCOCK MURDER CASE.

Mr. Baxt lives in New York, is a bachelor, and is devoted to his VCR.